A COLD CREEK CHRISTMAS STORY

BY
RAEANNE THAYNE

MILLS &
BOON

Published in Great Britain 2015
by Mills & Boon, an imprint of Harlequin (UK) Limited,
Eton House, 18-24 Paradise Road, Richmond, Surrey, TW9 1SR

© 2015 RaeAnne Thayne

ISBN: 978-0-263-25194-4

23-1215

Harlequin (UK) Limited's policy is to use papers that are natural, renewable and recyclable products and made from wood grown in sustainable forests. The logging and manufacturing processes conform to the legal environmental regulations of the country of origin.

Printed and bound in Spain
by CPI, Barcelona

Chapter One

If she didn't have thirty children showing up in the next half hour, Celeste Nichols would have been tempted to climb into her little SUV, pull out of the Pine Gulch library parking lot and just keep on driving.

She shifted the blasted endlessly ringing cell phone to the crook of her shoulder while she sorted through the books scattered across her cubicle in the offices of the library to find what she would be reading for story hour.

"I told you earlier in the week, I'm not ready to make a decision about this yet."

Joan Manning, her and Hope's long-suffering literary agent, gave a low, frustrated sound of disapproval. "We can't hold them off much longer. We've already stalled for two weeks. They want to start production right after the holidays, and they can't do that without signatures from you and Hope."

Celeste gazed down at a copy of Dr. Seuss's perennial holiday favorite, *How the Grinch Stole Christmas*. She had a feeling she was the one being the Grinch here. Hope was completely on board with the extraordinary offer one of the leading animation companies had made for movie rights to their book, *Sparkle and the Magic Snowball*.

Celeste was the one who couldn't quite be comfortable with the idea of someone else taking control of her words, her creation, and turning *Sparkle* into an animated movie, complete with the attendant merchandising and sublicensing. A fast-food chain was already talking about making a toy for its kids' meals, for crying out loud.

The whole journey of the past twelve months seemed like a bizarre, surreal, completely unbelievable dream.

A year ago she had known exactly who she was— an unassuming children's librarian in the small town of Pine Gulch, Idaho, in the western shadow of the Teton Mountain Range.

Now, to her immense shock, she was a celebrated author about to see the release of her second children's book with several more scheduled in the next few years. Along with that had come things she had never imagined when she'd been writing little stories for her niece and nephew—she had a website, a publicist, a literary agent.

Her quiet, safe world seemed to be spinning out of her control, and this movie deal was the prime example.

"A few more days, Celeste," Joan pushed. "You can't keep stalling. You have to make a decision. Hollywood has a short attention span and an even shorter supply of patience. Do you want your story made into a movie or not?"

She liked Joan very much, as brash and abrupt as the woman could be, but everything with her was an emergency and had to be decided *right now*. Pressure pains stabbed with little forks behind her eyes and her shoulders felt as if someone had jammed them in a vice and was cranking down hard.

"I know. I just need to be sure this is the right choice for Sparkle."

"Sparkle is a fictional character. You need to be sure it's the right choice for *you* and for your sister. We've been going over this for weeks. I don't know what else I can say to convince you this is the best deal you're going to get."

"I know that. You've done a great job with the negotiations. I just need…a little more time."

"A few days," Joan said, her voice clipped with frustration. "That's all, then I have to give them some kind of an answer."

"I know. Thank you. I'll get back with you tomorrow or the day after."

"Just remember, most people would see this as a dream come true."

Apparently, she wasn't *most people*. After they said their goodbyes, Celeste set her cell phone back on the desk, again fighting the urge to climb into her SUV and keep on driving.

That was her sister Hope's way, to wander from place to place as they had done in their itinerant childhood. Celeste was different. She liked security, consistency.

Normalcy.

In the past twelve months her life had been anything *but* normal. She had gone from writing only for herself and her niece and nephew to writing for a vast audience she never could have imagined.

It had all started when her sister Hope had come home

the previous Christmas for what was supposed to be a brief stay between overseas teaching jobs. Hope had over-heard her reading one of her stories to Louisa and Bar-rett and had put her considerable artistic skills to work illustrating the story to sell in the gift store of their fam-ily's holiday-themed attraction, The Christmas Ranch.

The result had been a sweet, charming Christmas story about a brave little reindeer named Sparkle. Nei-ther Hope nor Celeste had ever imagined the book would be touted by a presenter on one of the national morn-ing news program—or that the resulting sales would ex-plode internationally and end up saving the floundering Christmas Ranch *and* the family's cattle operation, the Star N Ranch.

She was beyond gratified that so many people liked her writing and the story—and especially Hope's delight-ful illustrations—but some part of her wanted to go back to that peaceful time when her biggest decisions revolved around what to read for her weekly story hour at the Pine Gulch Public Library.

With a sigh, she turned back to the job at hand. She was still sorting through the final choices when the head librarian poked her head into the cubicle.

"Looks as if we're going to have a nice crowd." Frankie Vittori, the head librarian, looked positively gleeful. "I hope we have room for everybody."

"Oh, that's terrific!" she exclaimed, mentally shelving her worries about the movie deal for now.

She meant the words. She loved nothing more than in-troducing children to the wonder and magic to be found inside the pages of a good book.

Books had saved her. During the chaos of her child-hood, they had offered solace and safety and *hope* amid fear. She had no idea how she would have survived without friends such as Anne of Green Gables, Bilbo Baggins, Matilda, Harry Potter and Hermione and Ron Weasley.

"I only hope we've got enough of our craft project to go around. It seems as if the crowd increases every month."

Frankie grinned. "That's because everybody in town wants to come hear our local celebrity author read in hopes of catching a sneak peek at the new Sparkle story coming down the pike."

She managed to conceal her instinctive wince. She really didn't like being a celebrity.

On one level, it was immensely gratifying. Who would have ever dreamed that she—quiet, awkward, introverted Celeste Nichols—would be in this position, having people actually *care* what she had to say?

On another, it was terrifying. At some point the naked emperor was always exposed. She feared the day when somebody would finally ask why all the fuss about her simple little tales.

For now, Frankie was simply thrilled to have a crowd at the library for any kind of reason. Celeste's boss and friend vibrated with energy, as she always did, her toe tapping to unheard music and her fingers fidgeting on the edge of the desk. Frankie was as skinny as a flagpole, probably because she never stopped moving.

Her husband, Lou, on the other hand, was the exact opposite—a deep reservoir of calm serenity.

They made the perfect pair and had two adorable kids who fell somewhere in the middle.

"I know it's more work for you," Frankie went on. "But I have to say, it's a brilliant idea to have two story times, one for the younger kids in the morning and one for early and middle readers after school."

Celeste smiled. "If you do say so yourself?"

Frankie beamed. "What can I say? I'm brilliant sometimes."

"That you are." Since Frankie had come to the library from upstate New York two years earlier, patron usage was way up and support had never been higher.

Frankie was bold and impassioned about the need for libraries, especially in the digital age. Celeste was more than a little envious of her overwhelming confidence, which helped the director fight for every penny of funding from the city council and the community in general.

Celeste would never be as outgoing and vivacious as Frankie, even though she was every bit as passionate about her job as the children's librarian. She liked being behind the scenes—except for the weekly story times, her favorite part of the job.

She checked her watch and quickly stood up. "I guess I'd better get out there."

She picked up the box of craft supplies they would use for the activity she had planned and headed for the large meeting room they had found worked best for story times.

"Oh, I almost forgot," Frankie said with a sly grin. "Make sure you check out the major hottie dad out there at ten o'clock."

Despite her amazing husband, Frankie was always locating hot guys, whether at their weekly lunches at one of the restaurants in town or on the few trips they'd taken into Jackson Hole or Idaho Falls. She always said she was only scouting possible dates for Celeste, which made Celeste roll her eyes. Her last date had been months ago.

"Is he anybody I know?"

"*I've* never seen him before. He's either new in town or a tourist. You can't miss him. He's wearing a Patek Philippe watch and a brown leather jacket that probably costs as much as our annual nonfiction budget. He's definitely not your average Cold Creek cowboy with horse pucky on his boots."

Okay, intriguing. She hadn't heard of anybody new moving into the small town, especially not someone who could afford the kind of attire Frankie was talking about. Sometimes well-to-do people bought second or third homes in the area, looking for a mountain getaway. They built beautiful homes in lovely alpine settings and then proceeded to visit them once or twice a year.

"I'll be sure to check him out while I'm trying to keep the kids entertained."

Frankie was right about one thing—the place was packed. Probably thirty children ranging in age from about six to eleven sat on the floor while roughly that same number of parents sat in chairs around the room.

For just an instant she felt a burst of stage fright at the idea of all those people staring at her. She quickly pushed it down. Normally she didn't like being in front of a crowd, but this was her job and she loved it. How could she be nervous about reading stories to children? She would just pretend their parents weren't there, like she usually did.

When she walked in, she was heartened by the spontaneous round of applause and the anticipation humming in the air.

She spotted a few people she recognized, friends and neighbors. Joey Santiago, nephew to her brother-in-law Rafe, sat beside his father, waving wildly at her.

She grinned and waved back at him. She would have

thought Rafe was the hot dad—all that former navy SEAL mojo he had going on—but Frankie knew him well and he wasn't wearing a leather jacket or an expensive watch anyway.

She loved Rafe dearly, for many reasons—most important because he adored her sister Hope—but also because she wasn't sure she would be standing here, ready to entertain a group of thirty children with the magic of literature if not for his role in their lives so many years ago.

She saw a few other hot dads in the crowd—Justin Hartford, who used to be a well-known movie star but who seemed to fit in better now that he had been a rancher in Cold Creek Canyon for years. Ben Caldwell, the local veterinarian, was definitely hot. Then there was the fire chief, Taft Bowman, and his stepchildren. Taft always looked as though he could be the December cover model on a calendar of yummy firefighters.

All of them were locals of long-standing, though, and Frankie knew them well. They couldn't be the man she was talking about.

Ah, well. She would try to figure out the mystery later, maybe while the children were making the snowman ornaments she had planned for them.

"Thank you so much for coming, everybody. We're going to start off with one of my favorite Christmas stories."

"Is it *Sparkle and the Magic Snowball*?" Alex Bowman, Taft's stepson, asked hopefully.

She blushed a little as everyone laughed. "Not today. Today we're focusing on stories about Christmas, snow and snowmen."

Ben's son raised his hand. "Is Sparkle going to be here today, Ms. Nichols?"

Was that why so many people had turned out? Were they all hoping she'd brought along the *actual* Sparkle, who was the celebrity in residence at The Christmas Ranch?

Last year, Hope had talked her into having their family's beloved reindeer—and the inspiration for her eponymously named series of stories—make a quick appearance in the parking lot of the library.

"I'm afraid not. He's pretty busy at The Christmas Ranch right now."

She tried to ignore the small sounds of disappointment from the children and a few of their parents. "I've got tons of other things in store for you, though. To start out, here's one of everyone's favorite holiday stories, *How the Grinch Stole Christmas.*"

She started reading and, as usual, it only took a few pages before a hush fell over the room. The children were completely enthralled—not by her, she was only the vehicle, but by the power of story.

She became lost, too, savoring every word. When she neared the climax, she looked up for dramatic effect and found the children all watching her with eager expressions, ready for more. Her gaze lifted to the parents and she spotted someone she hadn't seen before, a man sitting on the back row of parents with a young girl beside him.

He had brown hair shot through with lighter streaks, a firm jaw and deep blue eyes.

This had to be the hot dad Frankie had meant.

Her heart began to pound fiercely, so loud in her ears she wondered if the children could hear it over the microphone clipped to her collar.

She knew this man, though she hadn't seen him for years.

Flynn Delaney.

She would recognize him *anywhere*. After all, he had been the subject of her daydreams all through her adolescence.

She hadn't heard he was back in Pine Gulch. Why was he here? Was he staying at his grandmother's house just down the road from the Star N? It made sense. His grandmother, Charlotte, had died several months earlier and her house had been empty ever since.

She suddenly remembered everything else that had happened to this man in the past few months and her gaze shifted to the young girl beside him, blonde and ethereal like a Christmas angel herself.

Celeste's heart seemed to melt.

This must be her. His daughter. Oh, the poor, poor dear.

The girl was gazing back at Celeste with her eyes wide and her hands clasped together at her chest as if she couldn't wait another instant to hear the rest of the story.

Everyone was gazing at her with expectation, and Celeste realized she had stopped in the middle of the story to stare at Flynn and his daughter.

Appalled at herself, she felt heat soak her cheeks. She cleared her throat and forced her attention back to the story, reading the last few pages with rather more heartiness than she had started with.

This was her job, she reminded herself as she closed the book, helping children discover all the delights to be found in good stories.

She wasn't here to ogle Flynn Delaney, for heaven's sake, even when there was plenty about him any woman would consider ogle-worthy.

* * *

Flynn didn't think he had ever felt quite so conspicuously out of place—and that included the times he had walked the red carpet with Elise at some Hollywood premiere or other, when he had invariably wanted to fade into the background.

They all seemed to know each other and he felt like the odd man out. Was everybody staring? He didn't want to think so, but he seemed to feel each curious sidelong glance as the residents of Pine Gulch tried to figure out who he was.

At least one person knew. He was pretty sure he hadn't imagined that flicker of recognition in Celeste Nichols's eyes when she'd spotted him. It surprised him, he had to admit. They had only met a few times, all those years ago.

He only remembered her because she had crashed her bike in front of his grandmother's house during one of his visits. Charlotte hadn't been home, so Flynn had been left to tend her scrapes and bruises and help her get back to the Star N up the road.

Things like that stuck in a guy's memory bank. Otherwise he probably never would have made the connection between the author of his daughter's favorite book, *Sparkle and the Magic Snowball*, and the shy girl with long hair and glasses he had once known in another lifetime.

He wouldn't be here at the library if not for Celeste, actually. He had so much work to do clearing out his grandmother's house and really didn't have time to listen to Dr. Seuss, as great as the story might be, but what other choice did he have? Since leaving the hospital, Olivia had been a pale, frightened shadow of the girl she used to be. Once she had faced the world head-on, daring and curious and funny. Now she was afraid of so many things. Loud noises. Strangers. Crowds.

From the moment she'd found out that the author of her favorite book lived here in Pine Gulch where they were staying for a few weeks—and was the children's librarian, who also hosted a weekly story hour—Olivia had been obsessed with coming. She had written the date of the next event on the calendar and had talked of nothing else.

She was finally going to meet the Sparkle lady, and she couldn't have been more excited about it if Celeste Nichols had been Mrs. Santa Claus in the flesh.

For the first time in weeks she showed enthusiasm for something, and he had jumped at the chance to nurture that.

He glanced down at his daughter. She hadn't shifted her gaze away from Celeste, watching the librarian with clear hero worship on her features. She seemed utterly enchanted by the librarian.

The woman was lovely, he would give her that much, though in a quiet, understated way. She had big green eyes behind her glasses and glossy dark hair that fell in waves around a heart-shaped face.

She was probably about four years younger than his own thirty-two. That didn't seem like much now, but when she had crashed her bike, she had seemed like a little kid, thirteen or so to his seventeen.

As he listened to her read now, he remembered that time, wondering why it seemed so clear to him, especially with everything that had happened to him since.

He'd been out mowing the lawn when she'd fallen and had seen her go down out of the corner of his gaze. Flynn had hurried to help her and found her valiantly trying not to cry even though she had a wide gash in her knee that would definitely need stitches and pebbles imbedded in her palm.

He had helped her into his grandmother's house and called her aunt Mary. While they'd waited for help, he had found first-aid supplies—bandages, ointment, cleansing wipes—and told her lousy jokes to distract her from the pain.

After Mary had taken her to the ER for stitches in her knee and he had finished mowing for his grandmother, he had gone to work fixing her banged-up bike with skills he had picked up from his mother's chauffeur.

Later that day, he had dropped off the bike at the Star N, and she had been almost speechless with gratitude. Or maybe she just had been shy with older guys; he didn't know.

He had stayed with his grandmother for just a few more weeks that summer, but whenever he had seen Celeste in town at the grocery store or the library, she had always blushed fiercely and offered him a shy but sweet smile.

Now he found himself watching her intently, hoping for a sight of that same sweet smile, but she seemed to be focusing with laser-like intensity on the books in front of her.

She read several more holiday stories to the children, then led them all to one side of the large room, where tables had been set up.

"I need all the children to take a seat," she said in a prim voice he found incongruously sexy. "We're going to make snowman ornaments for you to hang on your tree. When you're finished, they'll look like this."

She held up a stuffed white sock with buttons glued on

to it for eyes and a mouth, and a piece of felt tied around the neck for a scarf.

"Oh," Olivia breathed. "That's so cute! Can I make one, Dad?"

Again, how could he refuse? "Sure, if there are enough to go around."

She limped to a seat and he propped up the wall along with a few other parents so the children each could have a spot at a table. Celeste and another woman with a library name badge passed out supplies and began issuing instructions.

Olivia looked a little helpless at first and then set to work. She seemed to forget for the moment that she rarely used her left hand. Right now she was holding the sock with that hand while she shoved in pillow fluff stuffing with the other.

While the children were busy crafting, Celeste made her way around the tables, talking softly to each one of them.

Finally she came to them.

"Nice job," she said to his daughter. Ah, there it was. She gave Olivia that sweet, unguarded smile that seemed to bloom across her face like the first violets of springtime.

That smile turned her from a lovely if average-looking woman into a breathtaking creature with luminous skin and vivid green eyes.

He couldn't seem to stop staring at her, though he told himself he was being ridiculous.

"You're the Sparkle lady, aren't you?" Olivia breathed.

Color rose instantly in her cheeks and she gave a surprised laugh. "I suppose that's one way to put it."

"I love that story. It's my favorite book *ever*."

"I'm so happy to hear that." She smiled again, though he thought she looked a little uncomfortable. "Sparkle is pretty close to my heart, too."

"My dad bought a brand-new copy for me when I was in the hospital, even though I had one at home."

She said the words in a matter-of-fact tone as if the stay had been nothing more than a minor inconvenience. He knew better. She had spent two weeks clinging to life in intensive care after an infection had ravaged her system, where he had measured his life by each breath the machines took for her.

Most of the time he did a pretty good job of containing his impotent fury at the senseless violence that had touched his baby girl, but every once in a while the rage swept over him like a brushfire on dry tinder. He let out a breath as he felt a muscle flex in his jaw.

"Is that right?" Celeste said with a quick look at him.

"It's my very favorite book," Olivia said again, just in case Celeste didn't hear. "Whenever I had to do something I didn't want to, like have my blood tested or go to physical therapy, I would look at the picture of Sparkle on the last page with all his friends and it would make me feel better."

At Olivia's words, Celeste's big eyes filled with tears and she rocked back on her heels a little. "Oh. That's… lovely. Thank you so much for letting me know. I can't tell you how much that means to me."

"You're welcome," Olivia said with a solemn smile. "My favorite part is when Sparkle helps the animals with their Christmas celebration. The hedgehog is my favorite."

"He's cute, isn't he?"

The two of them gazed at each other in perfect charity

for a moment longer before a boy with blond hair and a prominent widow's peak tried to draw Celeste's attention.

"Ms. Nichols. Hey, Ms. Nichols. How do we glue on the hat?"

"I'll show you. Just a minute." She turned back to Olivia. "It was very nice to meet you. You're doing a great job with your snowman. Thanks for letting me know you enjoy the book."

"You're welcome."

When she left, Olivia turned back to her project with renewed effort. She was busy gluing on the button eyes when the woman beside Flynn finally spoke to him.

"You're new in town. I don't think we've met." She was blonde and pretty in a classic sort of way, with a baby on her hip. "I'm Caroline Dalton. This is my daughter, Lindy. Over there is my son, Cole."

He knew the Daltons. They owned much of the upper portion of Cold Creek Canyon. Which brother was she married to?

"Hello. I'm Flynn Delaney, and this is my daughter, Olivia. We're not really new in town. That is, we're not staying anyway. We're here just for a few weeks, and then we're going back to California."

"I hope you feel welcome here. This is a lovely place to spend the holidays."

"I'm sure it is, but we're not really tourists, either. I'm cleaning out my grandmother's home so I can put it up for sale."

He could have hired someone to come and clean out the house. There were companies that handled exactly that sort of thing, but as he and Olivia were Charlotte's only surviving descendants, he'd felt obligated to go through the house himself.

"Delaney. Oh, Charlotte! She must have been your grandmother."

"That's right."

Her features turned soft and a little sad. "Oh, everyone adored your grandmother. What a firecracker she was! Pine Gulch just doesn't feel the same without her."

His *life* didn't feel the same, either. He hadn't seen her often the past few years, just quick semiannual visits, but she had been a steady source of affection and warmth in his chaotic life.

He had barely had the chance to grieve her passing. That bothered him more than anything else. He hadn't even been able to attend the memorial service members of her church congregation had held for her here. He had been too busy in the ICU, praying for his daughter's life.

"I miss her, too," he said quietly.

She looked at him with kindness and warmth. "I'm sure you do. She was an amazing person and I feel blessed to have known her. If you need help sorting through things, please let me know. I'm sure we could find people to give you a hand."

With only a little more than a week to go before Christmas? He doubted that. People were probably too busy to help.

He didn't bother to express his cynicism to Caroline Dalton. "Thanks," he said instead.

"Despite your difficult task, I hope you're able to find a little holiday spirit while you're here."

Yeah, he wasn't a huge Christmas fan for a whole slew of reasons, but he saw no reason to share that with a woman he'd just met.

"Daddy, I can't tie the scarf. Can you help me?" Olivia asked.

She *could* use her left arm and hand. He'd seen her do it at therapy or when she lost herself in an activity, but most of the time she let it hang down uselessly. He didn't know how to force her into using it.

"Try again," he said.

"I can't. It's too hard," she answered plaintively. He sighed, not wanting to push her unnecessarily and ruin her tentative enjoyment of the afternoon.

He leaned down to help her tie the felt scarf just as Celeste made her way back around the table to them.

"I love that snowman!" she exclaimed with a smile. "He looks very friendly."

Olivia's answering smile seemed spontaneous and genuine. Right then Flynn wanted to hug Celeste Nichols on the spot, even though he hadn't talked to her for nearly two decades.

His little girl hadn't had much to smile about over the past few months. He had to hope this was a turning point, a real chance for her to return to his sweet and happy daughter.

At this point, he was willing to bring Olivia to the library every single day if Celeste could help his daughter begin to heal her battered heart.

Chapter Two

She was late.

By the time she helped the last little boy finish his snowman, ushered them all out of the meeting room and then cleaned up the mess of leftover pillow stuffing and fleece remnants, it was forty minutes past the time she had told her sisters to expect her.

They would understand, she was sure. Hope might tease her a little, but Faith probably wouldn't say anything. Their eldest sister saved her energy for the important things like running the cattle ranch and taking care of her children.

She stopped first at the foreman's little cottage, just down the driveway from the main house. It felt strange to be living on her own again after the past year of being back in her own bedroom there. She had moved back after her brother-in-law Travis died the previous summer so she could help Faith—and Aunt Mary, of course—with the children and the housekeeping.

Hope had lived briefly in the foreman's house until she and Rafe married this fall. After she'd moved into the house they purchased together, Faith and Mary had taken Celeste aside and informed her firmly that she needed her own space to create. She was a bestselling author now. While Faith loved and appreciated her dearly, she didn't want Celeste to think she had to live at the ranch house for the rest of her life.

Rather reluctantly, she had moved to the foreman's cottage, a nice compromise. She did like her own space and the quiet she found necessary to write, but she was close enough to pop into the ranch house several times a day.

As she walked inside, her little Yorkie, Linus, rolled over with glee at the sight of her.

She had to smile, despite her exhaustion from a long day, the lingering stress from the phone call with Joan and the complete shock of seeing Flynn Delaney once more.

"How was your day?" she asked the little dog, taking just a moment to sink onto the sofa and give him a little love. "Mine was *crazy.* Thanks for asking. The weirdest I've had in a long time—and that's saying something, since the entire past year has been surreal."

She hugged him for a moment. As she might have predicted, a sleek black cat peeked her head around the corner to see what all the fuss was about.

Lucy, who had been with her since college, strutted in with a haughty air that only lasted long enough for her to leap onto the sofa and bat her head against Celeste's arm for a little of the same attention.

The two pets were the best of friends, which helped

her feel less guilty about leaving them alone during the day. They seemed to have no problem keeping each other company most of the time, but that didn't stop them from exhibiting classic signs of sibling rivalry at random moments.

She felt her tension trickle away as she sat in her quiet living room with her creatures while the Christmas tree lights that came on automatically gleamed in the gathering darkness. Why couldn't she stay here all evening? There were worse ways to spend a December night.

Linus yipped a little, something he didn't do often, but it reminded her of why she had stopped at the house.

"I know. I'm late. I just have to grab Aunt Mary's present. Give me a second."

She found the gift in her bedroom closet, the door firmly shut to keep Lucy from pulling apart the tissue paper inside the gift bag.

"Okay. I'm ready. Let's go."

Linus's tail wagged with excitement, but Lucy curled up on the sofa, making abundantly clear her intent to stay put and not venture out into the cold night.

"Fine. Be that way," she said, opening the door for the dog. The two of them made their way through lightly falling snow to the ranch house, a sprawling log structure with a steep roof and three gables along the front. Linus scampered ahead of her to the front door. When she opened it, the delicious scents of home greeted her—roast beef, potatoes and what smelled very much like cinnamon apple pie.

As she expected, her entire family was there, all the people she loved best in the world. Aunt Mary, the guest of honor, was busy at the stove stirring something that smelled like her heavenly brown gravy. She stepped aside to let Faith pull a pan of rolls out of the oven as Hope helped the children set the table, where her husband, Rafe, sat talking with their neighbor Chase Brannon.

The children spotted Linus first. They all adored each other—in fact, the children helped her out by letting him out when they got home from school and playing with him for a little bit.

"There you are," Faith exclaimed. "I was beginning to worry."

"Sorry. I sent you a text."

Faith made a face. "My phone ran out of juice sometime this afternoon, but I didn't realize it until just now. Is everything okay?"

Not really, though she wasn't sure what bothered her more—the movie decision she would have to make in the next few days or the reappearance of Flynn Delaney in her world. She couldn't seem to shake the weird feeling that her safe, comfortable world was about to change.

"Fine," she said evasively. "I hope you didn't hold dinner for me."

"Not really. I was tied up going over some ranch accounts with Chase this afternoon, and we lost track of time."

"Fine. Blame me. I can take it," Chase said, overhearing.

"We always do," Hope said with a teasing grin.

Chase had been invaluable to their family since Faith's husband died, and Celeste was deeply grateful to him for all his help during the subsequent dark and difficult months.

"I'm happy to blame you, as long as that means I wasn't the cause of any delay in Aunt Mary's birthday celebration," Celeste said with a smile as she headed for her great-aunt.

She kissed the woman's lined cheek as the familiar scent of Mary's favorite White Shoulders perfume washed over her. "Happy birthday, my dear. You are still just as stunning as ever."

Mary's grin lit up her nut-brown eyes. "Ha. Double sevens. That's got to be lucky, right?"

"Absolutely."

"I don't need luck. I've got my family around me, don't I?"

She smiled at them all and Celeste hugged her again, deeply grateful for her great-aunt and her great-uncle Claude, who had opened their hearts to three grieving, traumatized girls and gave them a warm haven and all the love they could need.

"We're the lucky ones," she murmured with another hug before she stepped away.

For all intents and purposes, Mary had been her mother since Celeste turned eleven. She had been a wonderful one. Celeste was all too aware that things could have been much different after their parents died if not for Mary and Claude. She and her sisters probably would have been thrown into the foster care system, likely separated, certainly not nurtured and cared for with such love.

She had a sudden, unexpected wish that their mother could be here, just for a moment, to see how her daughters had turned out—to meet her grandchildren, to see Hope so happily settled with Rafe, to see the completely unexpected success of their Sparkle book.

December always left her a little maudlin. She supposed that wasn't unexpected, considering it had been the month that had changed everything, when she, her sisters and their parents had been hostages of a rebel group in Colombia. Her father had been killed in the rescue effort by a team of US Navy SEALs that had included Rafe Santiago, who was now her brother-in-law.

She wouldn't think about that now. This was a time of celebration, a time to focus on the joy of being with her family, not the past.

She grabbed a black olive out of a bowl on the counter and popped it in her mouth as she carried the bowl to the table.

"I talked to Joan this afternoon," she told Hope.

"I know. She called me, too. I reminded her that any decision about making a movie had to be made jointly between us, and each of us had veto power. Don't worry, CeCe. I told her firmly that I wouldn't pressure you. You created the Sparkle character. He belongs to you."

That wasn't completely true and both of them knew it. She might have written the words, but it was Hope's illustrations that had brought him to life.

"I don't know what to do," she admitted as Faith and Mary joined them at the table carrying bowls and trays of food.

"Your problem has always been that you analyze everything to death," Mary pointed out. "You know someone is going to make a Sparkle movie at some point. It's as inevitable as Christmas coming every year. People love the story and the characters too much. If you like this production company and think they'll do a good job with it based on their reputation, I don't know why you're dragging your feet."

Mary was right, she realized. She was overthinking, probably because she was so concerned with making the right decision.

She hated being afraid all the time. She knew it was a by-product of the trauma she and her sisters had endured at a young age, but neither Hope nor Faith seemed as impacted as she had been.

Hope seemed absolutely fearless, spending years wandering around underdeveloped countries with the Peace Corps, and then on her own teaching English. Faith had plowed all her energy and attention into her family—her marriage, her children, the ranch.

Celeste's life had become her job at the library and the stories she created.

In some ways, she supposed she was still a hostage of Juan Pablo and his crazy group of militants, afraid to take a move and embrace her life.

"Everything's ready and I'm starving," Mary said cheerfully. "What are we waiting for? Let's eat."

Dinner was noisy and chaotic, with several different conversations going at once.

"How did story time go?" Faith asked when there was a lull in the conversation.

She instantly remembered the shock of looking up from Dr. Seuss to see Flynn and his daughter.

"Good." She paused. "Charlotte Delaney's grandson, Flynn, and his daughter were there. I guess he's in town to clean out Charlotte's house."

"Flynn Delaney." Hope made a sound low in her throat. "I used to love it whenever he came to stay with Charlotte. Remember how he used to mow the lawn with his shirt off?"

Celeste dropped her fork with a loud clatter, earning her a curious look from Hope.

"Really?" Rafe said, eyebrow raised. "So all this time I should have been taking my shirt off to mow the lawn?"

Hope grinned at him. "You don't *need* to take your shirt off. You're gorgeous enough even when you're wearing a parka. Anyway, I was a teenage girl. Now that I'm older and wiser I prefer to use my imagination."

He shook his head with an amused look, but Celeste was certain his ears turned a little red.

"You said Flynn came into the library with his daughter," Faith said, her voice filled with compassion. "That poor girl. How is she?"

Considering Flynn's connection to Charlotte, whom they all had loved, everyone in Pine Gulch had followed the news reports. Celeste thought of Olivia's big, haunted eyes, the sad, nervous air about her.

"Hard to say. She limped a little and didn't use her left arm while we were doing the craft project, but other than that she seemed okay."

"Who is Flynn Delaney and what happened to his daughter?" Rafe asked.

"It was all over the news three or four months ago," Chase said. "Around the time Charlotte died, actually."

"You remember," Hope insisted. "We talked about it. He was married to Elise Chandler."

Understanding spread over Rafe's handsome features. "Elise Chandler. The actress." He paused. "Oh. That poor kid."

"Right?" Hope frowned. "What a tragedy. I saw on some tabloid in the supermarket that Flynn never left her side through the whole recovery."

Somehow that didn't seem so surprising, especially considering his devotion to his daughter during story time.

"What happened to her?" Louisa asked. At eleven, she was intensely interested in the world around her.

Her mother was the one who answered. "Elise Chandler was a famous actress," Faith said. "She was in that superhero movie you loved so much and a bunch of other films. Anyway, she was involved with someone who turned out to be a pretty messed-up guy. A few months ago after a big fight, he shot Elise and her daughter before shooting and killing himself. Even though she was injured, Olivia managed to crawl to her mother's phone and call 911."

Celeste had heard that 911 call, which had been made public shortly after the shooting, and the sound of that weak, panic-stricken voice calling for help had broken her heart.

"She seems to be doing well now. She didn't smile much, but she did tell me she loves the Sparkle book and that her dad used to read it to her over and over again in the hospital."

"Oh, how lovely!" Hope exclaimed. "You should take her one of the original Sparkle toys I sewed. I've still got a few left."

"That's a lovely idea," Mary exclaimed. "We definitely should do something for that poor, poor girl. It would have broken Charlotte's heart if she'd still been alive to see Flynn's little girl have to go through such a thing."

"You *have* to take it over there," Hope insisted. "And how about a signed copy of the book and the new one that hasn't come out yet?"

Her heart pounded at just the *idea* of seeing the man again. She couldn't imagine knocking on his door out of the blue. "Why don't *you* take it over? You're the illustrator! And you made the stuffed Sparkle, too."

"I don't even know him or his daughter."

"As if that's ever stopped you before," she muttered.

"It would be a really nice thing to do," Faith said.

"I baked an extra pie," Aunt Mary said. "Why don't you take that, too?"

All day long people had been pushing her to do things she didn't want to. She thought longingly of jumping in her SUV again and taking off somewhere, maybe Southern California where she could find a little sunshine. As tempting as the idea might be sometimes, she knew she couldn't just leave her family. She loved them to bits, even when they did pressure her.

She wanted to tell them all no, but then she thought of Olivia and her sad eyes. This was a small expenditure of effort on her part and would probably thrill the girl. "That's a very good idea," she finally said. "I'll go after dinner. Linus can probably use the walk."

"Perfect." Hope beamed at her as if she had just won the Newbery Medal for children's literature. "I'll look for the stuffed Sparkle. I think there's a handful of them left in a box in my old room."

What would Flynn think when she showed up at his house with a stuffed animal and an armful of books? she wondered as she chewed potatoes that suddenly tasted like chalk.

It didn't matter, she told herself. She was doing this for his daughter, a girl who had been through a terrible ordeal—and who reminded her entirely too much of herself.

Chapter Three

"Are you sure you don't want to help? This tinsel isn't going to jump on the tree by itself."

Flynn held a sparkly handful out to his daughter, who sat in the window seat, alternating between watching him and looking out into the darkness at the falling snowflakes.

She shook her head. "I can't," she said in a matter-of-fact tone. "My arm hurts too much."

He tried to conceal his frustrated sigh behind a cough. The physical therapist he had been taking her to since her injury had given him homework during this break while they were in Idaho. His assignment was to find creative activities that would force her to use her arm more.

He had tried a wide variety of things, like having Olivia push the grocery cart and help him pick out items in the store, and asking her help in the kitchen with slicing vegetables. The inconsistency of it made him crazy. Sometimes she was fine; other times she refused to use her arm at all.

After their trip to the library, he'd realized his grandmother's house was severely lacking in holiday cheer. She had made a snowman ornament and they had nowhere to hang it.

Any hope he might have harbored that she would show a little enthusiasm for the idea of decking their temporary halls was quickly dashed. She showed the same listless apathy toward Christmas decorations as she had for just about everything else except Celeste Nichols and her little reindeer story.

Other than hanging her own snowman ornament, she wasn't interested in helping him hang anything else on the small artificial tree he had unearthed in the basement. As a result, he had done most of the work while she sat and watched, not budging from her claim of being in too much pain.

He knew using her arm caused discomfort. He hadn't yet figured out how to convince an almost-seven-year-old she needed to work through the pain if she ever wanted to regain full mobility in her arm.

"Come on. Just take a handful and help me. It will be fun."

She shook her head and continued staring out at the falling snow.

Since the shooting, these moods had come over her out of nowhere. She would seem to be handling things fine and then a few moments later would become fearful, withdrawn and just want him to leave her alone.

The counselor she had seen regularly assured him it was a natural result of the trauma Olivia had endured.

He hated that each step in her recovery—physical and emotional—had become such a struggle for her.

After hanging a few more strands, he finally gave up. What was the point when she didn't seem inclined to help him, especially since he'd never much liked tinsel on trees anyway?

His father hadn't, either, he remembered. He had a stray memory of one of his parents' epic fights over it one year. Diane had loved tinsel, naturally. Anything with glitz had been right down her alley. Her favorite nights of the year had been red carpet events, either for her own movie premieres or those of her friends.

His father, on the other hand, had thought tinsel was stupid and only made a mess.

One night when he was about seven or eight, a few years before they'd finally divorced, his mother had spent hours hanging pink tinsel on their tree over his father's objections, carefully arranging each piece over a bough.

When they'd woken up, the tinsel had been mysteriously gone. As it turned out, Tom had arisen hours before anyone else and had pulled off every last shiny strand.

After a dramatic screaming fight—all on his mother's side—she had stormed out of their Bel Air house and hadn't been back for several days, as he recalled.

Ah, memories.

He pushed away the bitterness of his past and turned back to his daughter. "If you don't want to hang any more tinsel, I guess we're done. Do you want to do the honors and turn out the lights so we can take a look at it?"

She didn't answer him, her gaze suddenly focused on something through the window.

"Someone's coming," Olivia announced, her voice

tight. She jumped up from the window seat. "I'm going to my room."

He was never sure which she disliked more: large, unruly crowds or unexpected visitors showing up at the door. Nor was he certain she would ever be able to move past either fear.

With effort he forced his voice to be calm and comforting. "There's no reason to go to your room. Everything is fine. I'm right here. You're okay."

She darted longing little glances down the hall to the relative safety of her bedroom, but to her credit she sat down again in the window seat. When the doorbell rang through the house, Flynn didn't miss her instinctive flinch or the tense set of her shoulders.

He hoped whoever it was had a darn good excuse for showing up out of the blue like this and frightening his little girl half to death.

To his shock, the pretty librarian and author stood on the porch with a bag in her hand and a black-and-brown dog at the end of a leash. In the glow from the porch light he could see her nose and cheeks were pink from the cold, and those long, luscious dark curls were tucked under a beanie. She also wasn't wearing her glasses. Without the thick dark frames, her eyes were a lovely green.

"Hello." She gave him a fleeting, tentative smile that appeared and disappeared as quickly as a little bird hunting for berries on a winter-bare shrub.

"Celeste. Ms. Nichols. Hello."

She gave him another of those brief smiles, then tried to look behind him to where Olivia had approached. At least his daughter now looked more surprised and delighted than fearful.

"And hello, Miss Olivia," the librarian said. "How are you tonight?"

Her voice was soft, calm, with a gentleness he couldn't help but appreciate.

"Hi. I'm fine, thank you," she said shyly. "Is that your dog?"

Celeste smiled as the dog sniffed at Olivia's feet. "This is Linus. He's a Yorkshire terrier and his best friend is a black cat named Lucy."

"Like in *Charlie Brown's Christmas*!" She looked delighted at making the connection.

"Just like that, except Linus and Lucy are brother and sister. My Linus and Lucy are just friends."

Olivia slanted her head to look closer at the little dog. "Will he bite?"

Celeste smiled. "He's a very sweet dog and loves everybody, but especially blonde girls with pretty red sweaters."

Olivia giggled at this, and after another moment during which she gathered her courage, she held out her hand. The little furball licked it three times in quick succession, which earned another giggle from his daughter.

"Hi, Linus," she said in a soft voice. "Hi. I'm Olivia."

The dog wagged his tail but didn't bark, which Flynn had to appreciate given how skittish Olivia had been all evening.

She knelt down and started petting the dog—using her injured left arm, he saw with great surprise.

"He likes me!" Olivia exclaimed after a moment, her features alight with a pleasure and excitement he hadn't seen in a long time.

"Of course he does." Celeste smiled down at her with

a soft light in her eyes that touched something deep inside him.

"I'm sorry to just drop in like this, but I couldn't help thinking tonight about what you told me earlier, how the Sparkle book helped you in the hospital."

"It's my favorite book. I still read it all the time."

"I'm so happy to hear that. I told my sister, who drew all the pictures, and she was happy, too. We wanted to give you something."

"Is it for my birthday in three days? I'm going to be seven years old."

"I had no idea it was your birthday in three days!" Celeste exclaimed. "We can certainly consider this an early birthday present. That would be perfect!"

She reached into the bag and pulled out a small stuffed animal.

"That's Sparkle from the book!" Olivia rose to see it more closely.

"That's right. My sister made this while she was drawing the pictures for the first Sparkle book last Christmas. We have just a few of them left over from the original hundred or so she made, and I wondered if you might like one."

Olivia's eyes went huge. "Really? I can *keep* it?"

"If you want to."

"Oh, I do!" Almost warily, she reached for the stuffed animal Celeste held out. When it was in her hands, she hugged it to her chest as if afraid someone would yank it away.

For just a moment she looked like any other young girl, thrilled to be receiving a present. The sheer normalcy made his throat suddenly ache with emotions.

"He's *sooo* cute. I love it! Thank you!"

Olivia threw her arms around Celeste in a quick hug. Flynn wasn't sure if he was more shocked at her use of her injured arm or at the impulsive gesture. Like a puppy that had been kicked one too many times, Olivia shied away from physical touch right now from anyone but him.

Her therapist said it was one more reaction to the trauma she had endured and that eventually she would be able to relax around others and return to the sweet, warm little girl she once had been. He wondered if Dr. Ross ever would have guessed a stuffed reindeer might help speed that process.

Celeste probably had no idea what a rare gift she had just been given as she hugged Olivia back. Still, she looked delighted. "You're very welcome," she said. "You will have to come up to The Christmas Ranch sometime. That's where the real Sparkle lives."

Olivia stepped away, eyes wide. "The real Sparkle lives near here?"

"Just up the road." Celeste gestured vaguely in the direction of her family's place. "We've got a herd of about a dozen reindeer. Sparkle happens to be a favorite of my niece and nephew—of all of us, really. That's where I got the inspiration for the stories."

"Can we go see them, Dad? Can we?"

He shrugged. That was the thing about kids. They dragged you to all kinds of places you didn't necessarily want to go. "Don't know why not. We can probably swing that before the holidays."

Christmas was just around the corner and he was completely unprepared for it. He didn't like celebrating the holidays in the first place. He didn't really feel like hanging out at some cheesy Christmas moneymaking venture aimed at pouring holiday spirit down his throat like cheap bourbon.

But he loved his daughter, and if she wanted to go to the moon right now, he would figure out a way to take her.

"I like your tree," Celeste said, gazing around his grandmother's cluttered living room. "I especially like the tinsel. Did you help your dad put it up?"

A small spasm of guilt crossed her features. "Not really," she admitted. "My dad did most of it. I have a bad arm."

She lifted her shoulder and the arm in question dangled a little as if it were an overcooked lasagna noodle.

To her credit, Celeste didn't question how she could use that same arm to pet the dog or hold a stuffed reindeer.

"Too bad," she only said. "You're probably really good at hanging tinsel."

"Pretty good. I can't reach the high parts of the tree, though."

"Your dad helps you get those, right?"

"I guess."

Celeste picked up the bag of tinsel where Flynn had left it on the console table. "Can I help you put the rest of it up on the side you didn't get to yet? I'm kind of a tinsel expert. Growing up on The Christmas Ranch, I had to be."

Olivia looked at the tree, then her father, then back at Celeste holding the tinsel. "Okay," she said with that same wariness.

"It will be fun. You'll see. Sparkle can help. He's good at tinsel, too."

How she possibly could have guessed from a halftinseled tree that he had been trying to enlist his daughter's help with decorating, he had no idea. But he wasn't about to argue with her insight, especially when Olivia obediently followed her new heroine to the tree and reached for a handful of tinsel.

"Can I take your coat?" he asked.

"Oh. Yes. Thanks." She gave a nervous little laugh as she handed him her coat. At the library, she had been wearing a big, loose sweater that had made him wonder what was beneath it. She had taken that layer off apparently, and now she wore a cheerful red turtleneck that accentuated her luscious curves and made his mouth water.

He had an inkling that she was the sort of woman who had no idea the kind of impact she had on a man. As he went to hang her coat by the front door, he forced himself to set aside the reaction as completely inappropriate under the circumstances, especially when she was only trying to help his kid.

When he returned to the living room, he found her and Olivia standing side by side hanging tinsel around the patches of the tree he had left bare.

Her cute little dog had finished sniffing the corners of the room and planted himself on his haunches in the middle of the floor, where he could watch the proceedings.

Flynn leaned against the doorjamb to do the same thing.

How odd, that Olivia would respond to a quiet children's librarian and author more than she had her counselor, her physical therapist, the caregivers at the hospital. She seemed to bloom in this woman's company, copying her actions on the lower branches she could reach. While she still seemed to be favoring her injured arm, occasionally she seemed to forget it hurt and used it without thinking.

All in all, it wasn't a terrible way to spend a December evening while a gas fire flickered in Grandma Charlotte's fireplace and snowflakes fluttered down outside the window.

After several moments, the two of them used the last of the tinsel and Celeste stepped away to take in the bigger picture.

"That looks perfect!" she exclaimed. "Excellent job."

Olivia's smile was almost back to her normal one. She held up the stuffed animal. "Sparkle helped."

"I told you he would be very good at hanging tinsel."

Whatever worked, he figured. "Let me hit the lights for you," he said. "We can't appreciate the full effects with the lights on."

He turned them off, pitching the room into darkness except for the gleaming tree. The tinsel really did reflect the lights. His mom had been right about that, even if she had gotten so many other things wrong.

"Oh. I love it. It's the prettiest tree *ever*," Olivia declared.

"I have to agree," Flynn said. "Good job, both of you."

"And you," Olivia pointed out. "You did most of it earlier. We only filled in the gaps."

"So I did. We're all apparently excellent at decorating Christmas trees."

Celeste met his gaze and smiled. He gazed back, struck again by how lovely she was with those big green eyes that contrasted so strikingly with her dark hair.

He was staring, he realized, and jerked his gaze away, but not before he thought he saw color climb her high cheekbones. He told himself it must have been a trick of the Christmas lights.

"Oh, I nearly forget," she exclaimed suddenly. "I have another birthday present for you. Two, actually."

"You do?" Olivia lit up.

"Well, it's not actually your birthday yet, so I completely understand if you want to wait. I can just give them to your dad to hold until the big day."

As he might have predicted, Olivia didn't look all that thrilled at the suggestion. "I should open them now while you're here."

"I guess I should have asked your dad first."

He shrugged, figuring it was too late to stop the cart now. "Go ahead."

With a rueful, apologetic smile, she handed the bag to Olivia. "It's not wrapped, since I didn't know it was your birthday when I came over. I'm sorry."

His daughter apparently didn't care. She reached into the bag and pulled out a book with colorful illustrations on the cover.

"Ohhh," she breathed. "It's another *Sparkle and the Magic Snowball* book!"

"This one is signed by both me and my sister, who did the illustrations. I figured since it's your favorite book, you ought to have a signed copy."

"I love it. Thank you!"

"There's something else," Celeste said when his daughter looked as if she were going to settle in right on the spot to reread the story for the hundredth time.

Olivia reached into the bag and pulled out a second book. While it was obvious the artist had been the same, this had different, more muted colors than the original Sparkle book and hearts instead of Christmas ornaments.

"I haven't seen this one! *Sparkle and the Valentine Surprise.*"

"That's because it's brand-new. It's not even in stores yet. It's coming out in a few weeks."

"Dad, look!"

She hurried over to him, barely limping, and held out the book.

"Very nice. We can read it tonight at bedtime."

"I can't wait that long! Can I read it now?"

"Sure. First, do you have something to say to Ms. Nichols?"

Olivia gazed at the woman with absolute adoration. "Thank you *so much*! I just love these books and the stuffed Sparkle." Again, she surprised him by hugging Celeste tightly, then hurried to the window seat that she had claimed as her own when they'd first arrived at Charlotte's house.

He gazed after her for a moment, then turned back to Celeste.

"How did you just do that?" he asked, his voice low so that Olivia couldn't hear.

She blinked, confusion on her features. "Do what?"

"That's the first time I've seen her hug anyone but me in months."

"Oh." Her voice was small, sad, telling him without words that she knew what had happened to Elise and Olivia and about Brandon Lowell.

"I guess you probably know my daughter was shot three months ago and her mother was killed."

Her lovely features tightened and her eyes filled with sorrow. "I do. I followed the case, not because I wanted to read about something so terribly tragic, but because I...knew you, once upon a time."

Color rose on her cheeks again, but he had no idea why.

"She's been very withdrawn because of the post-traumatic stress. I haven't seen her warm up to anyone this quickly since it happened."

"Oh." She gazed at Olivia with a soft look in her eyes. "It's not me," she assured him. "Sparkle is a magic little reindeer. He has a comforting way about him."

He was quite certain Celeste was the one with the comforting way, especially as she had created the fictional version of the reindeer, but he didn't say so.

"Whatever the reason, I appreciate it. I had hoped bringing her here to Idaho where we can be away from the spotlight for a few weeks might help her finally begin to heal. It's good to know I might have been right."

The concern and love in his voice came through loud and clear. Flynn obviously was a devoted father trying his best to help his daughter heal.

Celeste's throat felt tight and achy. This poor little girl had watched her mother's life slip away. "She's been through a horrible ordeal. It might be years before the nightmares fade."

"You sound as if you know a little something about nightmares." He studied her closely.

She didn't want to tell him she *still* had nightmares from those terrible weeks in captivity and then their miraculous rescue with its tragic consequences. She had cried herself to sleep just about every night for weeks. In a second rapid-fire blow, just as the overwhelming pain of losing their father had begun to ease a little, their mother had lost her short but intense battle with cancer and they had come here to stay with Uncle Claude and Aunt Mary.

She couldn't tell him that. She barely knew the man,

and he had demons of his own to fight. He didn't need to share hers.

"Everybody has nightmares," she answered. "To paraphrase John Irving, you don't get to pick them. They pick you."

"True enough."

Her dog made a little whiny sound and started looking anxious, which meant he probably needed to go out.

"I need to take Linus home. Sorry again to drop in on you like this out of the blue."

He smiled a little. "Are you kidding? This has been the best thing to happen to us in a long time. She's completely thrilled. And thanks for helping with the Christmas tree. It looks great."

"You're welcome. If you need anything while you're here, my family is just a short walk away. Oh. I nearly forgot. This is for you."

She reached into the bag and pulled out the pie Aunt Mary had boxed up for easier transport.

"What is it?"

"My aunt makes amazing berry pies. She had an extra and wanted you to have it."

He looked stunned at the gesture. "That's very kind. Please give her my thanks."

"I'll do that." She reached for her coat but he beat her to it, tugging it from the rack so he could help her into it.

She was aware of him behind her again, the heat and strength of him, and her insides jumped and twirled like Linus when he was especially happy.

She was being ridiculous, she told herself. She wasn't a thirteen-year-old girl with a crush anymore.

She quickly shoved her arms through the sleeves and stepped away to tie her scarf.

"Are you sure you're okay walking home?" he asked. "Looks as if it's snowing harder. Let me grab my keys and we'll drive you home."

She shook her head, even as she felt a warm little glow at his concern. "Not necessary. It's not far. I like to walk, even in the snow, and Linus still has a little energy to burn off. Thank you, though."

He still looked uncertain, but she didn't give him a chance to press the matter. She returned to the living room doorway and waved at his daughter.

"Goodbye, Olivia. I hope you enjoy the book."

She looked up with that distracted, lost-in-the-story sort of look Celeste knew she wore frequently herself. "I'm already almost done. It's super good."

It was one thing in the abstract to know people enjoyed her work. It was something else entirely to watch someone reading it—surreal and gratifying and a bit uncomfortable at the same time.

"I'm glad you think so."

Olivia finally seemed to register that she had on her coat. "Do you really have to go?"

"I'm afraid so. I have to take Linus home or Lucy will be lonely."

To her surprise, Olivia set aside the book, climbed down from the window seat and approached to give her one last hug.

"Thank you again for the books and for the stuffed animal," she said. "It was the best birthday ever—and I haven't even had it yet!"

"I'm so glad."

"Goodbye, Linus," Olivia said. She knelt down to scratch the Yorkie again and Linus obliged by licking her face, which made her giggle.

When Celeste turned to go, she found Flynn shaking his head with astonishment clear on his handsome features. She remembered what he had said about Olivia not warming to many people since her mother's death, and she was deeply grateful she had made the small effort to come visit the girl.

"I hope we see you again," he said.

Oh, how she wished he meant for *his* sake and not for his daughter's. "I'm sure you will. Pine Gulch is a small place. Good night."

She walked out into the snowy December night. Only when she was halfway back to the Star N did she realize she didn't feel the cold at all.

Chapter Four

Over the weekend she tried not to think about Flynn and his sweet, fragile daughter. It wasn't easy, despite how busy she was working an extra shift at the library and helping out in the gift shop of The Christmas Ranch.

Even the multiple calls she and Hope took from Joan about the movie development deal couldn't completely distract her random thoughts of the two of them that intruded at the oddest times.

She knew the basics of what had happened to Elise Chandler and her daughter at the hands of the actress's boyfriend, but she was compelled to do a few internet searches to read more about the case. The details left her in tears for everyone involved, even the perpetrator and his family.

Brandon Lowell obviously had been mentally ill. He had been under treatment for bipolar disease and, according to evidence after the shooting, had stopped taking his medication a month before, claiming it interfered with his acting abilities and the regular television role he was playing.

He never should have had access to a firearm given his mental health but had stolen one from Elise's bodyguard a few days before the shooting.

She found it a tragic irony that the woman used a bodyguard when she went out in public but had been killed by someone close to her using the very tool intended to protect her.

The whole thing made her so very sad, though she was touched again to read numerous reports about Olivia's dedicated father, how Flynn had put his thriving contracting business in the hands of trusted employees so he could dedicate his time to staying with his daughter every moment through her recovery.

None of that information helped distract her from thinking about him. By Monday afternoon, she had *almost* worked the obsession out of her system—or at least forced herself to focus on work as much as possible, until Frankie came in after a morning of online seminars.

"I figured out who he is!" her friend exclaimed before she even said hello.

"Who?"

"You know! The hot dad who came to story time last week. I spent all weekend trying to figure out why he looked so familiar and then this morning it came to me. I was washing my hair and remembered that shower scene in *Forbidden* when the hero washes the heroine's hair and it came to me. Elise Chandler! Sexy dad is her ex-husband. It has to be! That cute little girl must be the one who was all over the news."

Flynn must hate having his daughter be a household name, even though her mother certainly had been.

"Yes. Flynn Delaney. Charlotte Delaney, his grandmother, lived close to The Christmas Ranch and he used to come spend summers with her."

"You knew all this time and you didn't say anything?"

It wasn't her place to spread gossip about the man. Even now, just talking to her dear friend, she felt extremely protective of him and Olivia.

"I'm sure they would appreciate a little privacy and discretion," she said. "Olivia has been through a terrible ordeal and is still trying to heal from her injuries. I don't think they need everybody in town making a fuss over them."

"Oh, of course. That makes sense. That poor kid."

"I know."

"How is she doing?"

She thought of Olivia's excitement the other day when she had taken the books to her and that spontaneous, sweet embrace. "She's still got a long road but she's improving."

"I'm so glad."

"Olivia is apparently a big Sparkle fan, and that was the reason they came to the story time."

She had been touched several times to remember the girl telling her how much her book had helped during her recovery. Who would have guessed when she had been writing little stories for her niece and nephew that an emotionally and physically damaged girl would one day find such comfort in them?

To her relief, Frankie dropped the subject. Celeste tried once more to return to her work, vowing to put this ridiculous obsession out of her head. An hour later her hopes were dashed when Frankie bustled back to the children's section, her eyes as wide as if she'd just caught somebody trying to deface a book.

"He's here again!"

She looked up from the books she was shelving. "Who's here?"

"Hottie Dad and his cute little girl! Elise Chandler's poor daughter. They just walked in."

"Are you sure?"

"He's a hard man to miss," Frankie said.

Celeste's heartbeat kicked up several notches and her stomach seemed tangled with nerves. She told herself that was ridiculous. He wasn't there to see her anyway. Maybe he wouldn't even come back to the children's section.

"I wonder what they're doing here," Frankie said, her dark eyes huge.

It wasn't to see her, Celeste reminded herself sternly. She was a dowdy, shy librarian, and he couldn't possibly have any interest in her beyond her status as his daughter's favorite author.

"Here's a wild guess," she said, her tone dry. "Maybe they're looking for books."

Frankie made a face. "He doesn't have a library card, does he?"

"Probably not," she acknowledged. "They're only here for a few weeks, then they'll be returning to California."

The thought was more depressing than it should have been.

"Well, ask him if he wants a temporary one while he's here."

Why did *she* have to ask him anything? She wanted to hide here in the children's section and not even have to face him. But a moment later Olivia limped in, Sparkle the stuffed reindeer in her hand along with the new book.

"Hi, Ms. Nichols! Hi!"

Celeste smiled at both of them. "Hello. It's lovely to see you today. Happy birthday!" She suddenly remembered.

"Thank you," Olivia said. "I begged and begged my dad to bring me to the library today."

"Did you?"

She held up Sparkle. "I had to tell you how much I liked the new book, just as much as the first one. Sparkle is *so funny*. I've read it about ten times already."

"Wow. That's terrific. Thanks for letting me know."

"And my dad read it to me twice and he laughed both times. He hardly *ever* laughs."

"Not true," he protested. "Okay, it's true that I laughed at the book. It's hilarious. But it's not true that I hardly ever laugh. I don't know where you came up with that. I laugh all the time. I'm a freaking hyena."

Celeste laughed out loud, which earned her a surprised look from Frankie.

"You're so lucky that you had the chance to read the new book," Frankie informed her. "Half the children in town would willingly forgo all their presents under the tree if they could lay their hands on the next Sparkle book."

Even though she was grossly exaggerating, the library director had the perfect tone with Olivia—friendly and polite, but not overly solicitous. She had a feeling Flynn would hate the latter.

"It's really, really good," Olivia said solemnly. "I still like the first one best, but the second one is almost my favorite."

Frankie smiled, but before she could answer, one of the other library volunteers came over with a question about checking out DVDs, and she reluctantly excused herself to deal with the crisis.

"Is there something I can help you with?" Celeste asked after her friend walked away. "Would you like a temporary card so you can check out materials? I'm sure that wouldn't be a problem, considering I know where to find you."

"No. Actually, we have another reason for being here."

If she wasn't mistaken, Flynn looked a little uncomfortable, which made her even more curious.

"Oh? What is it?"

He didn't answer and Olivia didn't say anything, either. Finally Flynn nudged her. "Go ahead."

"It's my birthday," the girl began.

"I know. I think it's great that you decided the library is the perfect place to celebrate a birthday. I completely agree!"

Olivia giggled a little. "No, we're not celebrating my birthday here. I told my dad the only thing I want for my birthday is to have pizza."

"Ooh, pizza. My favorite," she said, though she was still mystified about why they might be at the library and why Flynn still looked uncomfortable. "Are you looking for a book on how to make pizza?"

The girl shook her head. "We're going to the pizza restaurant down the street."

"I can highly recommend it. It's one of my favorite places."

Olivia gave her a shy look. "That's good. Because I want to have pizza with *you* on my birthday."

She blinked, taken by surprise. "With…me?"

"Yes. That would be the best birthday ever. My favorite thing to eat and my new friend and the lady who writes such good Sparkle books." She beamed as if the matter was settled.

"Don't feel obligated," Flynn said quickly. "If you already have plans, we completely understand. Isn't that right, Olivia?"

"Yes," the girl said.

Dinner. With Olivia and Flynn. She thought of a hundred reasons why she should say no. How could she possibly eat with these nervous butterflies racing around in her stomach? And she probably wouldn't be able to think of anything to say and would look even more stupid than she felt.

All those reasons paled into insignificance. Olivia wanted to have pizza with her for her birthday, and Celeste couldn't let her own social awkwardness stand in the way of making that particular wish come true.

"I would be honored to come help you celebrate your birthday. Thank you for inviting me."

Olivia's smile was sweetly thrilled. "She said yes, Dad!"

The sight of this tough-looking man gazing down at his daughter with such love just about broke Celeste's heart. "So I heard. That's great." He turned to her. "What time are you finished with work?"

"Five-thirty."

"Would seven work for pizza? We can pick you up."

"I can meet you at the restaurant."

"We don't mind. Do you still live at the Star N?"

She knew he probably didn't mean for that to sound pitiful, but she still had to wince. That wasn't exactly true. She had gone off to Boise for her undergraduate work, then Seattle for her master's degree. She wasn't *completely* a homebody, even if she had jumped at the chance to return to her hometown library to work.

If she was living on her family's ranch, it wasn't because of any failure to launch, only because of the tragic circumstances of Travis's death.

"I live on the ranch but not in the main house," she told him. "I'm at the foreman's place, the small log house closest to the entrance."

"Perfect. Plan on us at seven."

She was going out to dinner with Flynn Delaney and his daughter. This certainly wasn't the way to get the man out of her head, but she didn't see how she could refuse.

The truth was she didn't want to anyway. She was both touched and flattered that sweet Olivia wanted to spend time with her for her birthday.

"Sounds good. Meanwhile, are you sure you don't want to check out some books on a temporary library card? We still have a great selection of holiday books available. It's the section there against the wall."

"Can we?" Olivia asked her father.

"Just a few," he said with a reluctant nod. "It might be tough to keep track of more than that while we're clearing out Grandma Charlotte's house."

Olivia headed immediately toward the Christmas storybooks, leaving Flynn alone with Celeste—or at least as alone as they could be in a public library.

A few moms she knew were browsing through the children's section with their toddlers, and she was pretty sure she caught more than one appreciative glance in his direction. As Frankie said, he was a hard man to overlook.

"Thanks for agreeing to come with us," Flynn said.

"It probably wasn't fair to spring that on you out of the blue. I would have called first, but I didn't have a phone number. I guess I could have found the number for the library, but I didn't think about it until we pulled up."

"It's fine."

"Seriously, you made her day. She has been asking me all afternoon if you could come to her birthday celebration. I didn't want to disappoint her. It's still pretty tough for me to deny her anything these days."

She couldn't imagine almost losing a child. The fear must have been overwhelming.

"I'm touched, if you want the truth. I don't believe I've ever been anyone's birthday wish before."

A strange glint appeared in his gaze, an expression she couldn't quite identify. After a moment he smiled. "Face it. You sealed your fate the other day when you showed up in person with a new book *and* a cute stuffed toy. You're now officially the coolest person in town."

She had to laugh at that ridiculous statement. "If that's the case, you both need to get out and meet more people in Pine Gulch."

Amusement crinkled the corners of his eyes. "We won't be here long enough to move in social circles around here. Anyway, I think Olivia and I are both quite happy with those we have already met in Pine Gulch."

Her heartbeat seemed to accelerate all over again at the teasing note in his voice. Her gaze met his and he was smiling at her with a warm look in his eyes that sucked away any ability she might have had to offer a semi-intelligent response.

To her relief, one of the moms came over to ask her a question about the puppet-book packages they lent out—

probably more to get a closer look at Flynn, she suspected, than out of any genuine quest for information.

He moved away to join his daughter while she picked a few other books and the moment was gone.

He had to finish taking care of things at his grandmother's house and get out of Pine Gulch.

As Flynn drove the short distance from Charlotte's house to the Star N Ranch, he was aware of a low, insistent unease. This town was growing on him, sucking him in.

He had always enjoyed coming here as a kid to spend time with his grandmother. The setting was beautiful, nestled against the Tetons, with pine forests and crystal clear streams.

The pace here seemed so very different from his childhood home in Southern California, quieter, gentler somehow. Almost like a foreign country, without convertibles and palm trees and self-absorbed celebrities.

He always felt a sense of peace settle over him the moment he passed through the city limits into town.

He thought he loved it here because of Charlotte, because she was such a steady source of love and support despite the chaos of the rest of his world. When he came to Pine Gulch, there were no raging fights that could go on for days, no slamming doors, no screaming voices. Only his calm, funny, laughing grandmother, with her colorful aprons and her bright smile and her small, tidy house beside the Cold Creek.

She was gone now, but he was aware of that same peace seeping through him, so very welcome after the terrible past few months.

It didn't make sense, he knew. He was only here to

finish taking care of Charlotte's house, not to find some kind of peace.

That was part of the reason he was so drawn to Celeste Nichols, he acknowledged as he neared her family's ranch. She had a calming way about her that drew him to her.

He couldn't imagine any two people more different than Celeste and Elise—the sweet children's librarian and author and the passionate, flamboyant, ambitious actress.

His marriage had been a mistake from the beginning. After growing up with a mother in the entertainment business—and a father who had hated it—and seeing the neuroses and the superficiality of that way of life, he had wanted no part of it.

After high school and college, he had set his business degree aside and obtained a contractor's license instead. After only a few years his construction company had established a reputation for quality and dependability. Then at one of his mother's frequent parties, he had met a stunning—and hungry—young actress.

She had pursued him aggressively, and he—like probably most guys in their early twenties—had been too flattered to use his brain. In his lust-addled state, it had taken him several weeks to realize she was more interested in his connection to his mother and her powerful Hollywood circle than in him.

But by then Elise had become pregnant, despite the precautions they had taken. He had done what he thought was right and married her, but it had been the ultimate exercise in futility. Both of them had known from the beginning it would never last. The two years before she had filed for divorce had been among the toughest of his life, sweetened only by his complete adoration for his baby girl.

Everything he did, then and now, was for Olivia. That was the only reason he was driving to pick up Celeste Nichols right now, not because of this powerful attraction he hadn't been able to shake since that first day in the library.

What was it about her? Yes, she was pretty in a calm, buttoned-down kind of way with those lovely dark-fringed green eyes and dark curls. She had an understated loveliness she seemed to be doing her best to hide from the world.

His entire life he had been surrounded by beautiful women who were empty shells once a guy broke through the surface to the person inside. Despite their short acquaintance, he was certain Celeste wasn't like that.

Her kindness to Olivia touched him. He tried to tell himself that was the reason for this strange reaction to her. It was gratitude; that was all.

Somehow he wasn't buying it as he passed the entrance to The Christmas Ranch on his way to the Star N.

"What is that place?" Olivia asked, gazing out the window at the colorful holiday display they could see from the road.

"It's a place where people pay money to help find the Christmas spirit," he explained. "They have different activities here like sledding, sleigh rides, that kind of thing."

"Look, Dad! That sign says Home of the Real Sparkle," she read. "That must be where he lives! Can we pay the money and see him and maybe do some of the other stuff? The sledding and stuff?"

Her request took him by surprise, especially considering how apathetic she had been about decorating their house for Christmas. She hadn't summoned much energy at all for celebrating this year. He couldn't blame her after what she had endured, but it was one more thing that broke his heart, especially considering how excited she had been about the holiday season in years past.

Maybe Celeste Nichols and her reindeer book were rubbing off on Olivia.

"We'll have to see. I thought you weren't very interested in Christmas this year."

"I guess we could do a *few* Christmas things," she said slowly. "Whether we do them or not, Christmas is coming anyway."

"True enough." For a girl who had just turned seven, she could be remarkably wise sometimes. She was tough and courageous, he told himself. Even if she was struggling now, she would make it through this eventually.

"Is this where Celeste lives?" Olivia asked when he pulled up in front of the little house not far from the bigger Star N ranch house.

"That's what she said. The foreman's house."

"Look. She has a Christmas tree, too."

Since her family ran The Christmas Ranch, he would have been more shocked if she *didn't* have one.

"I wonder if I can see her cute little dog, Linus."

"I wouldn't be a bit surprised," he told her.

Olivia opened the passenger door almost before he had the SUV in Park, and she raced up the driveway without him, only limping a little. While he was still unbuckling his seat belt, she was already at the doorbell, and by the time he reached the door, Celeste had opened it and was greeting his daughter.

"Of course," she was saying. "You can absolutely come in and meet Lucy the cat. She loves new friends."

Apparently his daughter had invited herself inside. He rolled his eyes but followed her when Celeste held open the door for both of them.

The house wasn't large, perhaps only eight or nine hundred square feet. The living room was decorated in a casual, comfortable style, heavy on bright colors, with lots of plump pillows and books. The Christmas tree was about the only holiday decoration, he was surprised to see.

"Nice place," he said.

"Thanks. I just moved over a few months ago from the main house, but so far I've been enjoying it. I'm close enough to help out with my niece and nephew when my sister Faith needs me. At the same time, I'm far enough away from the chaos that I can write. I've even got my own writing space in the second bedroom."

"It's comfortable."

She smiled. "I like it."

Her furry-faced little dog scampered in from the kitchen, followed by an elegant-looking black cat, who watched them carefully from the doorway as if trying to determine whether they were friends or foes.

"Hi, Linus." Olivia sank to the floor to pet the dog. After a moment, the cat sidled over.

"That's Lucy," Celeste said. "She can be a little snooty at first, but once she warms up, she'll be your best friend. Just give her a moment."

Sure enough, while Olivia mostly paid attention to the small dog, the cat moved closer and closer until she rubbed her head against Olivia's leg.

"I think she likes me," she whispered.

"I'm sure of it," Celeste said with a smile.

"Looks as if you need to pick up a pet or two," she said to Flynn in an undertone.

"Don't give her any ideas," he said in the same low voice. Their gaze met and he felt a strange jolt in his gut at the impact of those green eyes behind the glasses.

"You don't want a little dog?"

He shrugged. When he was a kid, the only pets had been his mother's annoying, yippy little purse pooches. He had never really thought seriously about it before, too busy with work and his shared custody of Olivia.

When things settled down for her a little, maybe he would think about it. She did seem to be enjoying Celeste's pets.

Both he and Celeste seemed content to watch her petting the two pets, and he was aware of that elusive sense of peace seeping in again.

"How's the house cleaning going?" she asked him.

He thought of the work still ahead. "I don't think I realized what an undertaking it was to clear out eighty-five years of living. After about three days of work, we got one of the rooms cleared out today."

"Good work." She paused. "If you need help, I'm available most evenings."

She looked embarrassed after she spoke, though he wasn't quite sure why, when he took the offer as nothing but generous and kind, especially in the hustle-bustle of the holidays.

"Thank you," he said sincerely.

She gazed at him for a moment, then shifted her attention back to Olivia, but not before he saw a hint of color climb her cheeks.

"What are you doing with your business in California while you're here?"

"I'm doing as much as I can long-distance, but it hasn't been easy. Since the shooting, I've basically had to trust my second-in-command to take much of the load at the sites. I've been handling the administrative things after Olivia goes to bed. Everyone who works for me has been great. I couldn't ask for better people in my company, but I think we're all ready for things to start getting back to normal after the holidays."

She looked between him and his daughter, her expression soft. "You're a good father, Flynn. Olivia is lucky to have you."

"I don't know about that," he muttered. "A good father would have known what was going on at her mother's house. I should have seen it. It wasn't a stable situation for a young girl. Elise had boyfriend after boyfriend traipsing in and out of their lives, all tabloid fodder. Brandon Lowell at least had stuck around for longer than a few months. I was stupidly grateful for that, but if I had been paying more attention, I would have seen his downward spiral. Maybe I could have stepped in earlier."

"What would you have done?"

"I don't know. Found him the help he needed, at the very least. Maybe filed for an emergency custody order so we could have avoided all this trauma and pain." The nightmare of the shooting was as vivid and stark as if it had happened the day before. "Elise called me right before it all went south."

"She did?"

He checked to be sure Olivia wasn't paying attention to them but to the animals before he continued. "She told me Brandon had been drinking all day and was acting strangely. She was worried about him, but she didn't sound panicked or anything, was just calling to ask my advice. She'd done this before, called me for advice when he was drinking too much or having a manic episode, but something told me this time was different. I was on a job site fifty miles away, so I told her to grab Olivia and take her to my house, and I would deal with the situation when I got back."

He was quiet, regret a harsh companion. "I wish to hell she had listened to me. She was always so stubborn, thinking she knew best. I was about five miles from her place when I got the call from the police. I'll never forget that instant when it felt as if the whole world changed."

Chapter Five

She couldn't imagine what he must have gone through, knowing his daughter had been hurt. She also could tell by the threads of guilt twining through his voice that he blamed himself for not being able to control the situation and keep his daughter safe.

"What happened wasn't your fault," she murmured.

"Wasn't it?" he asked, the words clipped.

Unable to resist the need to offer him comfort, she reached out her hand and rested it softly on his.

She completely understood where he was coming from. She knew all about that crushing weight of responsibility.

In that last panicked rush toward the helicopter and the navy SEALs, she had been terrified as usual. She had hesitated, frozen in fear. Her father had paused to go back for her and shoved her in front of him, pushing her forward with his usual words of encouragement as they had raced to safety.

He had thrust her into the helicopter ahead of him, but her split second of fear had had a terrible cost. Her father had been shot just before he would have been able to make it to safety.

If she hadn't been so afraid, if she had started to run when he had first told her to go, maybe her father would still be with them now.

"Wouldn't it be wonderful if we were all given one do-over in life?" she murmured. "One free pass to go back and change one action, one decision, one thoughtless word?"

He gave her a searching look, as if trying to figure out what moment she would alter. Finally he nodded. "One would be a start, I suppose, though I probably could use about a half dozen free passes."

"Instead, we have to do our best to live with the consequences of our choices."

"Not an easy task, is it?"

No. She had been trying for nearly twenty years.

He flexed his hand and she realized with great chagrin that she was still touching him. She pulled her fingers back quickly, her skin still tingling from the heat of him.

After an awkward moment, he turned to his daughter.

"Olivia, we should probably take off or someone else will eat our delicious pizza."

"We haven't ordered it yet," she said with a concerned frown. "Do you think they'll run out?"

"I was just teasing. But we really should go."

"Okay," she said reluctantly. She rubbed noses with Linus and petted Lucy one last time, then stood up.

She might have been mistaken, but Celeste thought she seemed to be moving better, even than a few days before.

Flynn drove a luxury SUV that smelled of expensive leather with hints of his woodsy, intoxicating aftershave. As he drove to the pizza place in town, she and Olivia talked about the books the girl had checked out of the library and about her schoolwork and her home in California.

He seemed content to listen, though once or twice she caught him giving her a sidelong glance, no doubt trying to figure out how he had gotten saddled spending the evening with the boring children's librarian.

Monday night was family night at the Rocky Mountain Pizza Company—The Rock, as they called it in town. From the outside it looked as though the place was hopping.

This was one of the more family-friendly hangouts in Pine Gulch. Though it had a pool table in the back room, it also featured foosball and air hockey tables, as well as a few vintage video games like Ms. PAC-MAN and pinball.

Celeste came here about once a month, either with her sister or with friends. Usually she enjoyed the delicious wood-fired pizza and the comfortable, familiar atmosphere. The scent alone—garlic and yeast and a fabulous red sauce—made her stomach rumble.

On the heels of that first sensory overload, though, Celeste became aware that people were looking with curiosity at her and her companions.

She saw the police chief, Trace Bowman, and his wife, Becca, at one table with their children. In the next booth were Nate Cavazos and his wife, Emery, one of her good friends. Emery and Becca both looked intrigued.

For a wild moment, she wished she had refused the

invitation from Olivia—or that she had persuaded Flynn to take them all the way to Jackson Hole or even Idaho Falls, somewhere far away from Pine Gulch where people didn't know her.

Instead, she squared her shoulders, waved at her friends and did her best to ignore their speculative looks.

"Hi, Celeste," Natalie Dalton, the hostess chirped the greeting while looking at Flynn and Olivia with curiosity.

She used to babysit for Nat and her siblings. "Hi, Natalie. Great to see you. I miss seeing you at the library these days."

"I still come in, though mostly at night for study groups. I just don't have much reason to hit the children's section anymore unless I've got one of the little ones with me."

Her father and stepmother had two children together, in addition to the four Wade Dalton had had with his first wife, who had died tragically in childbirth.

Natalie turned her attention to Olivia and Flynn. "Hi, there. Welcome to The Rock. I don't think we've met. I'm Natalie."

Celeste felt as though she had the manners of a dried-up turnip right now. "Sorry. This is Flynn Delaney and his daughter, Olivia."

She smiled at them both. "Hi, Olivia. Hi, Flynn."

"We're here celebrating a certain young lady's seventh birthday today," Celeste said.

"Happy birthday!" Natalie exclaimed, beaming at her and holding her hand out for a fist bump.

"Thank you," Olivia said. She didn't meet her eye, and though she raised her hand halfheartedly to bump Nat's, she quickly lowered it again and looked at the floor.

What had happened to the animated birthday girl

who had chattered in the car about her favorite Jan Brett Christmas book? Now she seemed nervous and uneasy, as if she wanted to be anywhere else in the world than the best pizza place in the entire region.

Celeste placed a comforting hand on her shoulder. When she'd first arrived in Pine Gulch after their Colombian ordeal, it had taken her a long time before she could completely relax in public places like this. She imagined Olivia was feeling the same way.

"I've got the perfect table for a birthday girl," Natalie said, her cheerfulness undeterred by Olivia's reticence. "Follow me, guys."

Indeed, she led them to an excellent table overlooking the Christmas lights on Main Street. From here, they even could see the fun display in the window of the local toy store.

"Thanks," Flynn murmured. Olivia slid into the booth first and Flynn went in after her. Celeste slid across from them.

"What's good here?" Flynn asked, scanning one of the menus Natalie left them.

"Everything," she answered honestly. "The pizza, the pasta, the sandwiches. You can't go wrong."

"I wanted pizza," Olivia said, her voice still small.

"Pizza it is," Flynn said. "Why don't we order three personal size? Then everybody can choose the toppings they like."

"The personal size is usually huge," she told him. "At least enough for two people."

"That's okay. Pizza leftovers are one of the true joys in life, right?"

When he smiled, she thought *he* should have been the movie star in the family instead of his mother and former wife. He would break hearts all over the world with those completely natural good looks.

Her stomach jumped all over the place again. Oh, this crush was *so embarrassing*. She would be lucky if she could eat any pizza at all.

At least she was able to talk casually when he asked her to help him choose between pizza selections. A few moments later the server, Lucy Boyer—Natalie's cousin—headed over to take their order.

She beamed when she spotted Celeste. "Hey, Ms. N. How are things?"

"Great, Lucy. How are you?"

"Can't complain. I'm working on my college essays and it's such a pain. You probably love that kind of thing, since you're a genius author and all. You might not know this, but for some people writing is *hard*."

She didn't want to burst that particular fantasy by telling her the truth, that sometimes every single word was a struggle.

"Hey, what's this I hear about a Sparkle movie in the works?"

How on earth did rumors spread like that? She hadn't made her final decision yet, though she knew she couldn't wait much longer.

"A movie?" Olivia exclaimed. "Really?"

For some reason, Flynn's easy expression had tightened, and he was gazing at her with his brow furrowed.

"I don't know yet. Possibly." Probably.

She still wasn't sure she wanted to see her baby on the big screen, but at this point she didn't know how to stop that particular train.

"That's seriously cool. I'll be the first in line to buy tickets. That's such a great story."

"It's my favorite, too," Olivia said.

"Cool! I heard from a little squirrel that you've got a birthday today."

Olivia nodded. She looked as though she was torn between withdrawing into herself to hide from the attention and any kid's natural excitement about being the star of the day.

"We'll make sure your pizza is perfect, then. What kind do you want?"

Olivia ordered cheese, which Lucy assured them would come with a special birthday surprise. Celeste picked her favorite, margherita, which came with fresh basil and the hand-pulled mozzarella The Rock was famous for, and Flynn went for the meat lover's delight.

After she left, Flynn picked up the conversation.

"A movie?" he asked.

"We're in talks," she answered. "It's a terrifying proposition, to be honest."

"Will the real Sparkle be in the movie?" Olivia asked.

Celeste smiled. "It's going to be animated, so no."

She and the little girl started talking about their favorite holiday films—Olivia's was *Elf*, while Celeste still favored *It's A Wonderful Life*.

In no time, their pizza arrived. Olivia's surprise was that her pizza was shaped like a Christmas tree.

The pizza was every bit as good as usual, cooked just right in the wood-fired oven.

Flynn apparently agreed. "Wow," he said after the first bite. "That's a good pie. If I'd known how good, we would have been eating here every night since we came to town."

"Doug and Jacinda DeMarco, the owners, are big on the artisan pizza scene. They make their own mozzarella and burrata and try to use locally sourced produce and meats wherever they can. They have an extensive greenhouse where they grow their own fresh herbs and vegetables year-round. It's quite an operation."

"Who would have thought I could find such a good pizza in the wilds of eastern Idaho?"

She smiled, proud of her little community. While it might be primarily a ranching town, Pine Gulch was gaining a reputation as a foodie destination and a magnet for artists.

"I understand they get customers from as far away as Jackson Hole who read about the pizza online and want to try a slice."

She was finishing her second slice when she spotted her friend Caidy Caldwell coming in with her husband, the local veterinarian, and their children. Caidy had grown up in Cold Creek Canyon and had been a friend for a long time. Celeste loved seeing her so happy with Ben.

When she spotted Celeste, she waved, said something to Ben and the kids, then headed in her direction.

"Hi, Celeste! I'm so glad I bumped into you. Great story time last week. The kids really enjoyed it."

"Thanks. It was great to see you there."

"I don't know how you always manage to find such absolutely charming stories—old favorites and then so many that no one has ever heard before."

"That's my job," she said with a smile. That was one of her favorite parts about it, seeking out the new and unusual along with the classics everybody expected and loved.

"You do it well," Caidy said. "Almost *too* well. We might have to quit coming to the library. Every time you read a new book the kids have to buy it."

"Because they're all so good." Her stepdaughter, Ava, had joined her.

"Right. But now the shelves of our home library are bulging."

"You can never have too many books," Celeste answered.

"That's what I always say," Ava exclaimed. She turned to Olivia. "Hi. I'm Ava Caldwell."

"Sorry. This is Flynn Delaney and his daughter, Olivia. Flynn, this is my friend Caidy Caldwell and her daughter, Ava. Ava also has a brother about your age named Jack and a new baby brother who is the cutest thing around, Liam."

As her friend smiled at the two of them, Celeste didn't miss the flash of recognition or sympathy in her gaze before she smoothly masked her reaction. Caidy obviously had followed the news stories and knew what had happened to the girl.

"I'm happy to meet you both," her friend said with a smile. "Welcome to Pine Gulch. I hope you're staying around for a while."

He shook his head. "I'm afraid not. Only until after the holidays."

"Well, you picked one of the best times of the whole year to be here. You won't find many prettier winter wonderlands than this part of Idaho."

"It's lovely," he agreed.

"I didn't mean to interrupt your dinner. I just needed to ask you again what time practice is tomorrow. I know you've told me a half dozen times but I swear Christmas makes my brain leak out of my ears."

"Four thirty sharp at the St. Nicholas Lodge at the ranch. We should be done by six thirty."

"Perfect. My kids are so excited about it."

Celeste had no idea how Hope had persuaded her to take on one more thing, in this case organizing a small program to be performed at an inaugural Senior Citizens Christmas dinner a few days before the holiday.

Hope's particular skill was getting Celeste to do things she ordinarily never would attempt—like publish her books and then agree to allow one of those books to be made into a movie.

"Olivia, if you're going to be here through Christmas, you should think about being in the play," Ava suggested.

Flynn tensed up at the idea, his jaw taut. To Celeste's surprise, Olivia only looked intrigued.

"I was in a play in school once. It was fun."

"This isn't a huge production," Celeste assured Flynn. "We're just doing a simple Christmas program. Everybody who wants to participate gets a part. We're mostly singing songs everybody already knows."

"Can I do it, Dad?"

He frowned. "We'll have to talk about that. We're pretty busy cleaning out the house. I don't know if we'll have time to go to practices and things."

"There are only three practices," Celeste said. "Tomorrow, Thursday night and Saturday morning, and then the show is Tuesday, the day before Christmas Eve. She would be more than welcome to come. The rehearsals and the show are all at the St. Nicholas Lodge at The Christmas Ranch, just five minutes from your place."

A Christmas program. With an audience, applause. The whole bit. He wanted to tell them all absolutely not, to grab his daughter and drag her out of here.

He'd had enough of performers to last him a lifetime.

His entire life, he had been forced to wait on the sidelines while the important females in his life sought fame and recognition. His mother had made it clear from the time he was old enough to understand that he could never be the most important thing in her life—not when her adoring public already held that honor.

Elise had pretended otherwise, but when it came down to it, he had been even less important to her, only a stepping-stone on her journey to success.

He didn't want Olivia anywhere near a stage or a movie set. So far she hadn't shown any inclination in that direction, much to his relief. He wanted to keep it that way.

He told himself he was being ridiculous. It was only a Christmas program, not a Broadway production. Still, he didn't want to offer her any opportunity to catch the performing bug.

She was still so fragile. While her physical wounds had mostly healed, emotionally and mentally she was still had a long journey.

Was he being too protective? Probably. Her therapist in California told him he needed to relax and let go a little. He didn't need to watch over her every single moment. Right now he had a tendency to want to keep her close, to tuck her up against him and make sure nothing terrifying or tragic ever touched her again.

That wasn't a healthy approach, either. He couldn't protect her from everything, even though he wanted to.

"Can I do it, Dad?" she asked again.

This was the same girl who freaked out in large crowds, who didn't like loud noises and who tended to panic if strangers tried to talk to her.

Did she seriously think she could handle being on-stage in front of a bunch of strangers?

"We can talk about it later," he said.

"Absolutely," Caidy said with a cheerful smile, though he thought he saw soft compassion in her gaze.

Did she know about what had happened to Olivia? Probably. Most of the damn world knew. It had led media reports around the world for a week, had been on the cover of all the tabloids and celebrity rags.

When an Oscar-nominated actress is gunned down by her equally famous if mentally ill boyfriend—who then shoots her young child before killing himself—people tended to pay attention.

If he thought he could come to this remote corner of Idaho and escape notice, he was delusional. He doubted he could find anywhere on the planet where the news hadn't reached.

Maybe he could have taken Olivia on an African safari or something, but even then he wouldn't have been surprised if people in the veld knew of Elise Chandler.

"It was nice to meet you," Ava said politely. "I hope we see you at rehearsal tomorrow."

His daughter needed friends, he thought again. They had always been important to her. Before everything happened, she always had been begging to have a friend over to use the pool or watch a movie.

Since her release from the hospital, she hadn't been interested in doing the normal things a seven-year-old girl would do. Ava Caldwell was older than his daughter, maybe eleven or twelve, but she seemed very kind. Maybe Celeste knew of some other likely candidates Olivia could hang out with while they were in town.

If it helped her interact with children around her age, would the Christmas program really be that bad?

Being a parent was a tough enough gig under the best of circumstances. Throw in the kind of trauma his daughter had endured and he felt as though he was foundering, trying to stay afloat in thirty-foot swells.

The Caldwells waved and headed for their table, and Flynn returned to his delicious pizza. The people at the Rocky Mountain Pizza Company knew what they were doing when it came to pie, he had to admit. Olivia, he saw, ate two pieces and even some of the family-style tossed salad, which seemed something of a record for her, given her poor appetite these days.

While they ate, they talked about Christmas and books and a couple of movies they had all seen. Three different times, people who came into the restaurant stopped at their booth to say hello to Celeste.

Olivia seemed to find that of great interest. "Do you know everybody who lives here?" she finally asked.

Celeste laughed, a light, musical sound. "Not even close, though it feels like it sometimes. When you live in a place for a long time you get to know lots of people. I've been in Pine Gulch since I was eleven—except for the years I was away in Boise and Seattle for school."

"Where did you live before that?" he asked, suddenly intensely curious about her.

He was even more curious when her cheerful features seemed to go still and closed. She didn't say anything for several long seconds, so long that he wasn't sure she was going to answer him at all.

"It didn't seem like a tough question," he said mildly.

"For you, maybe," she retorted. "You grew up in California with your mother after your parents divorced, and spent your summers here with Charlotte, right?"

How did she know that? he wondered. He only remembered meeting her a few times back when he would come to visit and didn't remember ever sharing that information with her. Maybe Charlotte had told her.

He gave her a close look but she seemed lost in her own thoughts.

"That's right," he answered. "And you?"

"No one specific place," she finally answered. "I lived all over the globe, if you want the truth. I was born in a hut in Ghana, and before I was eleven, I lived in about two dozen countries. My parents were missionaries who started health clinics in underserved places of the world. Before I came to Pine Gulch, we were living in Colombia."

Some kind of vague, unsettling memory poked at him, a whisper he had once heard about Celeste and her sisters. Something to do with a kidnapping, with her parents.

He couldn't put his finger on the details. What was it? Was that the reason for those secrets in her eyes, for the pain he sensed there?

He opened his mouth to ask her, but before he could a loud clatter echoed through the place as a server busing the table next to them dropped the bin of dishes.

At the sudden, unexpected sound, Olivia gave one terrified gasp and slid from her seat under the table.

Damn, he hated these moments when her PTSD took over. They left him both furious and profoundly sad. He took a breath and leaned down to talk her through it, but Celeste beat him to it. She reached down and gave Olivia's shoulder a comforting squeeze beneath the table.

"It's okay. You're okay. It was only dishes. That's all. I know you were startled, but you're safe, sweetheart."

Olivia was making little whimpering noises that broke his heart all over again.

"I don't like loud noises," she said.

"Especially when you don't expect them and don't have time to prepare. Those are the *worst*, right?"

To his shock, Celeste spoke with a tone of experience. He gazed at her, trying to remember again what he knew about her and her sisters.

"They are," Olivia said. Though she still sounded upset, he could no longer hear the blind panic in her voice.

"Why don't you come up and finish your pizza? If you want, I can ask Lucy about fixing you one of their best desserts. It's a big gooey chocolate-chip cookie they bake in the wood-fired oven and top with hand-churned ice cream. I think you'll love it. I know it's my favorite thing to eat when I've been startled or upset about something."

After another moment, Olivia peeked her head out from under the booth. "They're not going to make that sound again, are they?"

"I don't think so. That was an accident."

"I hope they don't have another accident," she answered in a small voice.

"If they do, your dad and I are right here to make sure nothing hurts you."

That seemed enough to satisfy her. His daughter slid back onto the seat. She still had a wild look in her eyes, and he noticed she edged closer to him and constantly looked toward Celeste for reassurance while they finished their pizza.

He didn't miss the protective expression Celeste wore

in return, an expression that turned *his* insides just as gooey as that chocolate-chip cookie she was talking about.

He couldn't let himself develop feelings for this woman, no matter how amazing she was with his child, he reminded himself.

He had to focus on his daughter right now. She was the only thing that mattered.

Chapter Six

"Is she asleep?" Celeste whispered an hour later, when they made the turn onto Cold Creek Road.

He glanced in the rearview mirror and could see Olivia curled into the corner, her eyes closed and her cheek resting on her hand.

"Looks like it." He pitched his voice low. "She's always been a kid who can sleep anywhere, especially when she's had a long day. Driving in the car has always knocked her right out. When she was going through the terrible twos and used to fight going to bed, I would strap her in her car seat and drive her around the block a few times. She always ran so hard that when she finally stopped, she would drop like a rock by the time we hit the first corner."

"Did she stay asleep?"

"Yeah. That was the amazing part. She never seemed

to mind when I unstrapped her from her car seat and carried her into the house to her bed. I was kind of sorry when she outgrew that phase and started sleeping in her own bed without a fuss."

Beside him, he caught a flash of white in the darkness as Celeste smiled a little. "I imagine she was an adorable toddler."

"Oh, she was. Scary smart and curious about everything."

He felt a sharp pang in his heart when he thought again about how much she had changed, how she had become so fearful and hesitant. Would the old Olivia ever return, or was this their new version of normal?

"I wish you could have known her three months ago. Before."

Celeste reached out to touch his arm briefly, like a little bird landing on a branch for only a moment before fluttering away again.

"She's a wonderful girl, Flynn. A terrible thing happened to her, yes, but she's already demonstrated what a survivor she is. Trust me. She'll get through it in time. She may always have those dark memories—nothing can take them away completely—but eventually she'll learn how to replace them with happier thoughts."

He glanced over at her. "Is that how you coped?"

He could sense her sudden fine-edged tension. "I don't know what you mean."

"What happened to you? I vaguely remember my grandmother saying something about you and your sisters enduring a terrible ordeal, but I've been racking my brain and can't remember what. I should. I'm sorry."

She was silent for a long time and he didn't press, just

continued driving through the quiet night through Cold Creek Canyon.

The creek here wound beside the road and through the trees, silvery in the moonlight. Tall pines and firs grew beside cottonwoods along the banks, at times almost forming a tunnel over the road. It was beautiful and mysterious at night with the snow fluttering gently against the windshield and the occasional house or ranchette decorated with Christmas lights.

She finally spoke when they were almost to the Star N. "It's a time of my life I don't like to think about," she murmured.

"Oh?"

She sighed. "I told you my parents moved us around the globe under sometimes difficult circumstances."

He nodded, wondering what her life must have been like without any kind of stable place to call home. Had she thrived there or had she always felt as if something were missing in her life?

She loved to read. Perhaps books had been her one constant friend through all the chaos and uncertainty.

"When I was eleven, we moved to Colombia to open a clinic in a small, undeveloped region. My parents were assured over and over that it was a safe area to bring their daughters."

"It wasn't?"

"The village where we lived might have been safe, but several in the region were not."

With reluctance he pulled up in front of her house, wishing he could keep driving. He shouldn't have worried. She didn't appear to notice where they were, that he had parked the vehicle and turned to face her. She hardly seemed aware he was there as she spoke, her features tight and her eyes focused on some spot through the windshield that he had a feeling wasn't anywhere close to eastern Idaho.

"We had been living in the village about six weeks when the clinic drew the attention of the local rebel leader in one of those unstable villages who happened to be in need of some extra cash to fund his soldiers. I guess Juan Pablo thought he could get a handsome sum in ransom if he kidnapped the crazy American do-gooders. The only trouble with that plan was that my parents weren't associated with any larger organization with deep pockets. They were free agents, I guess you could say. There was no money to pay a ransom and no one to pay it."

"What happened?"

"Juan Pablo didn't believe my parents when they insisted no one could pay a ransom. He thought if he held us long enough, the US government at least would step in, especially with the lives of three young girls at stake. We were held hostage for several weeks in a squalid prison camp."

What the hell had her parents been thinking, to drag three young girls all over the world into these unstable situations? He was all for helping others and admired those selfless people who only wanted to make a difference in the world, but not when it cost the well-being of their own children.

"Did someone eventually pay the ransom?"

She shook her head. "That was never one of the options. Juan Pablo was just too stupid or too blinded by greed to realize it. Instead, after we had been held for several weeks, a team of US Navy SEALs mounted an early-morning rescue."

She paused, her head bowed and her dark curls hiding

her features. When she spoke, her voice was low, tight with remembered pain.

"The rescue wasn't a complete success. My father was…shot by Juan Pablo's rebels while we were trying to escape. He died instantly."

"Oh, Celeste. I'm so sorry."

"You can see why I feel great empathy for Olivia and what she's going through. Seeing a parent die violently is a trauma no child should have to endure."

"I completely agree," he said. "Again, I'm so sorry."

She lifted one shoulder. "It happened. I can't change it. For a long time, I struggled to deal with the injustice of it all. My parents were only trying to help others and my father paid the ultimate price for his benevolence. I can't say I've ever really found peace with that or ever will, but I've been able to move forward. For what it's worth, I freaked out at loud noises for a long time, too. Probably a good year or two after the accident."

"You seem to handle them fine now."

She gave a small laugh. "I wouldn't be a very good children's librarian if I couldn't handle a little noise, believe me. I would have run screaming into the night after the very first story time."

"So how did you come to live with your aunt and uncle?" he asked.

She shifted her gaze to his for only a moment before she looked out the windshield again, as if she couldn't quite bear to make eye contact while she told the rest of the story.

"In possibly the cruelest twist of all, our mother was diagnosed with cancer shortly after we were rescued from Colombia. She had been sick for a while but hadn't sought the necessary medical care. She'd apparently suspected something was wrong before we were taken and had made an appointment for tests in Bogota in the days right around our kidnapping—an appointment she couldn't make, for obvious reasons. It was…an aggressive and deadly form of cancer. Largely because she didn't get the treatment she needed in a timely manner, she died four months later, after we came back to the States."

Unable to resist, he reached for her hand and held it in his for a moment, wishing he had the words to tell her how much he admired her.

So many people he knew would have pulled inside themselves and let the tragedy and injustice of it turn them bitter and angry at the world. Instead, she had become a strong, compassionate woman who was helping children learn to love words and stories, while she wrote uplifting, heartwarming tales where good always triumphed.

She looked down at their joined hands, and her lips parted just a little before she closed them and swallowed. "After our mother died, Uncle Claude and Aunt Mary opened their home and their hearts to us, and we've been here ever since."

"And thus you entered the world of Christmas extravaganzas."

This time her laugh sounded more natural—a sweet, spontaneous sound that seemed to slide through his chest and tug at his heart. He liked the sound of her laughter. It made him want to sit in this warm car with her all night while soft Christmas music played on the stereo and snow fluttered against the windshield and his daughter slept soundly in the backseat.

"There was no Christmas Ranch before we came here. Uncle Claude had the idea a year later. My sisters and I share the theory that he did it only to distract us because he knew the holidays would be tough for us without our parents, especially that first anniversary."

"You were kidnapped at Christmastime?" That only seemed to add to the tragedy of it, that people could cruelly and viciously use an innocent family for financial gain during a time that was supposed to be about peace on earth and goodwill toward men.

"Yes." She leaned back against the seat and gazed out at the snowflakes dancing against the windshield. "My mother and father would try to keep up our spirits during our captivity by singing carols with us and encouraging us to make up Christmas stories."

"Ah. And you've carried on their storytelling tradition."

"In my feeble way, I guess you're right."

"Not feeble," he protested. "*Sparkle and the Magic Snowball* is a charming story that has captured the hearts of children and parents alike."

She looked embarrassed. "Mostly because of Hope and her beautiful illustrations."

"And because the story is sweet and hopeful at a time when people desperately need that."

She shifted in the seat, her cheeks slightly pink in the low light.

"I never expected any of this. I only wanted to tell stories to my niece and nephew. I don't know if I would ever have found the courage to submit it to a publisher. I didn't, actually. If not for Hope, all the Sparkle stories would still be in a box under my bed."

He released her fingers, not at all sure he liked this soft tenderness seeping through him. "Your parents would be so proud of you. Who would have guessed when you were sharing stories with your parents and sisters while you were all hostages during a dark Christmastime that one day you would be a famous author?"

"Not me, certainly."

"Does writing make you feel closer to your parents?"

She stared at him for a long moment, her eyes wide. "I… Yes. Yes, it does. I never realized that until right this moment when you said it. Sometimes when I'm writing, I feel as if they're with me again, whispering words of comfort to me in the darkness."

It would be easy to fall for her. Something about her combination of vulnerability and strength tugged at him, called to him in a way no other woman ever had.

He didn't have *time* for this, he reminded himself sternly. His daughter needed all his attention right now while she tried to heal. He couldn't dilute that attention by finding himself tangled up with a lovely librarian, no matter how much he might want to be.

"I had better go," she said after a moment. Did she also sense the growing attraction between them? Was that the reason for that sudden unease in her expression? "You should get a certain exhausted birthday girl home to her bed. Besides that, Linus and Lucy are probably wondering what in the world I'm doing out here for so long."

"Of course."

With far more reluctance than he knew he should feel, he opened his door and walked around the vehicle through the lightly falling snow to her door.

The December night smelled of pine and smoke from a fireplace somewhere close. The familiar mingle of scents struck deep into his memories, of the happy times he used to spend here with his grandmother. She had been his rock, the one constant support in the midst of his chaotic family life.

He breathed in deeply as he opened her car door. As they walked to her house, he realized with shock that this was the most peaceful he had felt in weeks, since that horrible day when he'd pulled up to Elise's house to find sirens and flashing lights and ambulances.

"You don't have to walk me to the door, Flynn. This isn't a date."

He suddenly *wished* it had been a date, that the two of them had gone to dinner somewhere and shared secrets and stories and long, delicious kisses.

If it had been a date, he possibly could give into this sudden hunger to kiss her at the doorstep, to finally taste that lush mouth that had been tantalizing him all evening.

"I want to make sure you don't slip," he said. It wasn't exactly a lie, just not the entire truth. "Ice can be dangerous."

She said nothing, though he thought her eyes might have narrowed slightly as if she sensed he had more on his mind than merely her safety.

They both made it up the steps without incident, and it only took her a moment to find a key in her purse.

"Good night," she said after she unlocked her door. "Thank you for including me in Olivia's birthday celebration. It was an honor, truly."

"We were the lucky ones that you agreed to come. It was a dream come true for her, sharing delicious pizza with her favorite author."

"I imagine her dreams will become a little more lofty as she gets older, but I'm happy I could help with this one." She gave him a sidelong look. "I hope I see her at the rehearsal tomorrow for the Christmas program. She really seemed to be interested in participating, and we would love to have her. Don't worry. She'll have fun."

Damn. He had almost forgotten about that. The peace he had been feeling seemed to evaporate like the puffs of air from their breaths.

"Don't plan on her," he warned.

"Why not?" she asked with a frown.

He raked a hand through his hair. "She's been through a brutal experience. Would you have been ready for something like this right after your own trauma?"

"I don't know," she admitted. "But if I expressed any interest at all, my aunt and uncle would have been right in the front row, cheering me on."

"I'm not your aunt and uncle," he said, with more bite in his voice than he intended.

She froze for just a moment, then nodded, her sweet, lovely features turning as wintry as the evening. "I'm sorry. You're right. I overstepped."

Her words and the tight tone made him feel like an ass. She was only trying to help his child.

"I'm sorry," he said. "I just can't see how getting up in front of a bunch of strangers and singing about peace on earth will help a young girl suffering from PTSD."

"I suppose you're right. I will say that my parents firmly believed a person could ease her own troubles while helping others—or at least trying to see them in a different light. Living here with Uncle Claude and Aunt Mary only reinforced that message. They started The Christmas Ranch so my sisters and I could find comfort in the midst of our own pain by bringing the joy of the holidays to others. It worked for us. I guess I was hoping it would do the same for Olivia, but you're her father. It's ultimately your decision."

Talk about backing a guy into a corner. What was he supposed to do?

Olivia *had* expressed a desire to participate, the first time anything had sparked her interest in weeks. He certainly had the right as her father to make decisions about what he thought was best for her, but what if he was wrong? What if she truly did need this? How could he be the one to say no to her?

"Fine," he said reluctantly. "I'll bring her tomorrow. If she enjoys herself, she can come back. But if I believe this is at all stressing her, I'll immediately put an end to it."

She smiled and he was struck again by how lovely she was. Behind her quiet prettiness was a woman of true beauty; she just seemed determined to hide it.

"Oh, that's wonderful. We'll be thrilled to have her. We'll see you tomorrow afternoon, in the main lodge at the ranch. Do you know where it is?"

"I'll figure it out."

"Excellent. I'll see you both tomorrow, then."

He knew that idea shouldn't leave him with this bubbly anticipation.

"Good night. Thanks again for having dinner with us."

"You're welcome. It was truly my pleasure."

He started to leave and then, prompted by the impulse that had been coursing through him all evening, he reached forward and kissed her softly on the cheek, the light sort of kiss people gave to even their casual acquaintances in California.

She smelled delicious—of laundry soap and almonds and some kind of springtime flowers. It took him a moment to place her scent. Violets—sweet and fresh and full of hope.

Instantly, he knew this was a mistake, that he would be dreaming of that scent all night.

Her eyes, wide and shocked behind her glasses, were impossibly green. It would be easy—so very easy—to shift his mouth just a few inches and truly kiss her. For an instant the temptation was overwhelming, but he drew on all his strength and forced himself to step away.

"Good night," he said again. To his dismay, his voice sounded ragged.

"Yes," she answered with a dazed sort of look that he told himself was only surprise.

He didn't give himself the chance to explore if that look in her eyes might have some other source—like a shared attraction, for instance. He just turned around and headed down the steps of her porch and toward his vehicle and his sleeping child.

When she was certain Flynn was in his car, driving back down the lane toward the main road, Celeste moved away from the window and sank into her favorite chair. Lucy—all sleek, sinuous grace—immediately pounced into her lap. She took a moment to pet the cat, her thoughts twirling.

For a moment there she had been almost positive Flynn Delaney had been about to *really* kiss her. That was impossible. Completely irrational. She must have been imagining things, right?

Why on earth would he want to kiss *her*? She was gawky and awkward and shy, more comfortable with books and her fictional characters than she was with men.

They were from completely different worlds, which was probably one of the reasons she'd had such a crush on him when she was a girl. He represented the unattainable. His mother was a famous movie star, and he was certainly gorgeous enough that *he* could have been one, too, if he'd been inclined in that direction.

He had been married to Elise Chandler, for Pete's sake, one of the most beautiful women on earth. How could he possibly be interested in a frumpy, introverted *children's librarian*?

The absurdity of it completely defied reason.

She must be mistaken. That moment when he'd kissed her cheek and their gazes had met—when she'd thought she'd seen that spark of *something* kindling in his gaze—must have been a trick of the low lighting in her entryway.

What would it have been like to kiss him? *Really* kiss him?

The question buzzed around inside her brain like a particularly determined mosquito. She had no doubt it would have been amazing.

She was destined never to know.

She sighed, gazing at the lights of her little Christmas tree sparkling cheerily in the small space. If she weren't careful, she could end up with a heart as shattered as one of the ornaments Lucy liked to bat off the branches.

It would be so frighteningly easy for her to fall for him. She was already fiercely attracted to him and had been since she was barely a teenager. More than that, she liked and admired him. His devotion to Olivia and his concern for her were even more attractive to Celeste than those vivid blue eyes, the broad shoulders, the rugged slant of his jaw.

If he were to kiss her—truly kiss her—her poor, untested heart wouldn't stand a chance.

After a moment she pushed away the unease. This

entire mental side trip was ridiculous and unnecessary. He wasn't interested in her and he wouldn't kiss her, so why spend another moment fretting about it?

Still, she couldn't help wishing she never had encouraged him to allow Olivia to participate in the Christmas program at the ranch. He was only here for a few weeks. The likelihood that she would even *see* the man again would have been very slim if not for Olivia and the program, and then she could have let this hopeless attraction die a natural death.

No worries, she told herself. She would simply do her best to return things to a casual, friendly level for his remaining time in Cold Creek.

How hard could it be?

Chapter Seven

Dealing with thirty jacked-up children a week before Christmas was not exactly the best way to unwind after a busy day at work.

Celeste drew in a deep breath, let it out slowly and ordered herself to chill. The noise level inside the two-story St. Nicholas Lodge was at epic levels. In one corner, a group of third-grade boys tossed around a paper airplane one of them had folded. In another, two girls were singing "Let it Go" at the top of their lungs. Three of the younger boys were chasing each other around, coming dangerously close to the huge Christmas tree that was the focal point of the lodge.

All the children were so excited for Christmas they were putting off enough energy to power the entire holiday light displays of three counties.

How she was supposed to whip this frenzy into organized chaos she had no idea.

"Whose crazy idea was this again?" her sister said, taking in the scene.

She sent Hope an arch look. "Go ahead. Raise your hand."

Hope offered up a rueful smile. "Sorry. It seemed like a fun idea at the time, a way to keep the local kids engaged and involved and give their parents a little break for shopping and baking, with the payoff of a cute show for the senior citizens at the end. I suppose I didn't really think it through."

"How very unlike you," Faith said drily from Celeste's other side.

Faith's presence was far more of a shock to Celeste than the wild energy of the children. Their eldest sister was usually so busy working on the cattle-raising side of the business that she didn't participate in many activities at The Christmas Ranch.

Perhaps she had decided to stop by because Louisa and Barrett were participating. Whatever the reason, Celeste was glad to see her there. The past eighteen months had been so difficult for Faith, losing her childhood sweetheart unexpectedly. It was good to see her sister reaching outside her comfort zone a little.

"I guess I didn't expect them all to be so...jacked up." Hope couldn't seem to take her gaze away from the younger children, who were now hopping around the room like bunny rabbits.

"You obviously don't have children," Faith said.

"Or work in a children's library," Celeste added.

"All kids act as if they're on crack cocaine the whole week before Christmas," Faith continued. "How could you not know that?"

"Okay, okay. Lesson learned. Now we just have to do our best to whip them into shape. We can do this, right?"

At the note of desperation in Hope's voice, Celeste forced a confident smile. "Sure we can."

Though she had her own doubts, she wouldn't voice them to Hope. She was too grateful for her sister for bringing light and joy back to the ranch.

After Travis's death in a ranching accident, Celeste, Mary and Faith had decided to close The Christmas Ranch, which had been losing money steadily for years. It had seemed the logical course of action. The Star N had been all but bankrupt and the Christmas side of things had been steadily losing money for years.

The plan had been to focus on the cattle side of the Star N, until Hope came back from years of traveling. She put her considerable energy and enthusiasm to work and single-handedly brought back the holiday attraction.

Part of that success had come because of the Sparkle books, which still managed to astonish Celeste.

She would always be deeply grateful to Hope for reminding them all of the joy and wonder of the season. Helping her with this Christmas program was a small way to repay her for all her hard work on behalf of the family.

"We've got this," she said to her sisters with a firm smile that contained far more assurance than she really felt.

She stepped forward and started to clap her hands to gather the children around when the door opened and a couple of newcomers came in. She turned with a smile to welcome them and felt an actual physical jolt when she saw Flynn and Olivia.

Despite his agreement the night before, she had been

certain Flynn would end up not bringing Olivia. She had seen the clear reluctance in his eyes and knew he worried the girl wasn't ready for this sort of public appearance.

She was thrilled for Olivia's sake that he had changed his mind, even if it meant she would have to do her best to ignore her own reaction to him—and even though she wouldn't have been nearly as exhausted today if not for him.

Her night had been restless. She couldn't seem to shake the memory of that moment when he had kissed her cheek—the warmth of his mouth, the brush of his evening shadow against her skin, the delicious, outdoorsy scent of him.

She shivered now in remembered reaction.

"Are you cold?" Faith asked in a low voice.

No. Exactly the opposite. "I'm fine." The lie rolled out far more easily than she would have expected. She had never been very good at stretching the truth.

"That must be Flynn," Hope said in an undertone, following her gaze to the newcomers. "Wow. He's really filled out since he was a teenager. Where's a nice lawn to be mowed when we need it?"

Faith laughed aloud, something she did very rarely these days. She had become so much more sober since Travis died.

"Good luck with that, finding a patch of bare lawn in Idaho in December," Faith said. "Too bad you can't talk him into shoveling snow without his shirt."

That was an image Celeste didn't need to add to the others in her head. She felt herself color, then immediately regretted the reaction when her sisters both looked between her and Flynn with renewed interest. Drat. They were both entirely too perceptive. The last thing she needed was for either Hope or Faith to get any match-making ideas where Flynn was concerned.

She quickly left her annoying sisters and moved forward to greet the newcomers.

Olivia looked nervous, half hiding behind her father. She visibly relaxed when Celeste approached.

"Hi, Celeste."

"It's my favorite just-turned-seven-year-old. Hi."

"It's noisy in here," Olivia informed her in an accusing sort of voice, as if it was *Celeste's* fault all the children were so wild.

"I know. Sorry about that. We're just about to get started. Once we focus everybody's attention, things will calm down. How are you today?"

Olivia smiled a little. "Okay, I guess. My dad didn't want to bring me, but I asked him and asked him until he finally said yes."

"I'm so glad," she said.

She shifted her gaze finally to Flynn and found him watching her with an unreadable look. She was suddenly aware that she must look tousled and harried. She had come straight from work, stopping at home only long enough to let Linus out and yank her hair up into a messy bun. She wore jeans and her favorite baggy sweater, and she was pretty sure her makeup had worn off hours ago.

For just a moment, she wished she could be beautiful and sophisticated instead of what she was—boring.

"Hi," she said to him. To her dismay, her voice sounded breathless and nervous. "I wasn't sure you would come."

"Apparently my daughter is relentless. Kind of like someone else I know."

She had to smile at the slightly disgruntled note in his voice.

"This will be fun. You'll see. We're going to practice until about six thirty. If you have shopping to do or want to go back to work on your grandmother's house, you're welcome to return for her then. Actually, I could even drop her off. It's not far."

He looked around at the chaos of the jacked-up children and then back at his nervous daughter.

"I believe I'll stay, if you don't mind."

What if she *did* mind? What if the idea of him watching her for the next two hours made her more nervous than a turkey at Thanksgiving?

She didn't know what else she could do but nod. "Sure. Of course. There are sofas over by the fireplace where you can make yourself comfortable. If you'd rather be closer to the action here, feel free to bring over a chair."

"Thanks."

He then proceeded to take neither of those suggestions. Instead, he leaned against the wall, crossed his arms over his chest and turned his full attention in her direction.

"Right." She swallowed and glanced at her watch. They should have started practicing five minutes ago.

She clapped her hands loudly and firmly three times to grab everyone's attention and said in her most firm librarian voice. "By the count of ten, I need everybody to gather around me and freeze in your best Christmas statue pose. Ready? One. Two. Three…"

By the time she hit four, all thirty children—thirty-one now, including Olivia—had made their way to her and adopted various positions. Destry Bowman, one of the older girls, was stretched out on the floor pretending to be asleep. Cute little Jolie Wheeler looked as if she was trying to do a figure eight on skates. Her niece, Louisa, appeared to be reaching on tiptoes for something, and it took Celeste a moment before she realized she was trying to put ornaments on an invisible Christmas tree.

Olivia looked uncertain, standing nervously with her hands clasped in front of her.

Celeste gave her a reassuring smile and then turned her attention to the other children.

"Perfect. Statues, you can all relax now and sit down."

The children complied instantly and she smiled. They might be a wild bunch but she loved them all. Each was someone whose name she knew, either from being neighbors and friends with their parents or from church or her work at the library.

"Thank you! This is going to be great fun, you'll see. The senior citizens and your families are going to *love* it, trust me, and you'll have fun, too. Are you all ready to put together a great show for your families?"

"Yes!" they shouted as one.

"Let's get to it, then."

He never would have predicted it when he walked into chaos, but somehow the ragtag collection of hyperactive children had calmed down considerably and were working hard together.

Celeste had organized the children into small groups of five or six and assigned one older child to teach them the song or dance they were to perform. She in turn moved between the groups offering words of advice or encouragement, working on a lyric here or a dance move there.

He found it charming to watch, especially seeing her lose her natural reserve with the children.

Was that why she had become a children's librarian, because she was more comfortable interacting with them?

He was curious—but then he was curious about *everything* that had to do with Celeste Nichols.

Naturally, he kept a careful eye on his daughter, but she seemed to have relaxed considerably since they'd walked in. Just now she was talking and—yes!—even *laughing* with three children he'd heard call Celeste their aunt, a couple of boys about her age and a girl who appeared to be a few years older.

Had Celeste said something to them, somehow encouraged them to be especially welcoming to Olivia? He wouldn't have been surprised, but maybe they were as naturally compassionate and caring as their aunt. Whatever the reason, the children seemed to have gone out of their way to show kindness and help her feel more comfortable, which went a long way toward alleviating his own concerns.

He doubted anything could make him feel totally enthusiastic about Olivia performing in the little production, but it helped considerably to see her enjoying herself so much and interacting with her peers.

He wasn't sure he was ready to admit it, but Celeste might have been right. This little children's performance in a small community in Idaho might be exactly what Olivia needed to help her begin to heal from the horrors she had endured.

He finally relaxed enough to take a seat on one of the sofas by the fireplace and was reading through email messages from his office on his cell phone when one of the women Celeste had been talking with when he and Olivia arrived took a seat on the sofa across from him.

"Hi, Flynn. You probably don't remember me, but I'm Hope Santiago. Used to be Nichols. I'm Celeste's sister."

Ah. No wonder she had looked familiar, though she

only shared green eyes in common with her sister. Instead of Celeste's silky brown hair and quiet, restful loveliness, Hope Santiago was pretty in a Bohemian sort of way, with long, wavy blonde hair and a cluster of exotic-looking bracelets at her wrist.

He had met her before, he thought, back when he used to come here for the summers.

"Hello. Sure, I remember you. You're married now. Congratulations."

She gave a pleased-as-punch smile and gestured through the doorway to what looked like an office where a big, tough-looking dude with a couple of tats was speaking on a cell phone.

"That's my husband, Rafe. He and I run The Christmas Ranch together."

"The two of you must just be overflowing with Christmas spirit."

She chuckled. "We do our best. Thanks for letting your daughter participate in the show. It means a lot to Celeste."

He wasn't sure he had exactly "let" Olivia do anything. He'd been steamrollered into it, when all was said and done, but so far things seemed to be working out.

He shrugged. "It's for a good cause, right? Making some older people happy. That can only be a good thing, right?"

"Exactly." She beamed at him.

"You're the artist," he realized suddenly. "The one who took Celeste's Sparkle story and turned it into a book."

She nodded. "That's me," she answered.

"They're charming illustrations that go perfectly with the story," he told her. "I read the second book again to my daughter last night, for about the twentieth time in just a few days. It's every bit as sweet as the first one. The two of you make a great team."

She looked pleased at his words. "Thanks, but Celeste is the creative genius. I just took her fabulous story and drew little pictures to go with it. Any success the Sparkle book has seen is because of her story."

"That's funny. She said almost exactly the same thing about you and your illustrations."

"She would," she said with a laugh. "Don't make the mistake of thinking we're always adoring sisters, so sweet to each other we'll make your teeth hurt. We're not afraid to have it out. I think I've still got a little bald spot in the back of my head where she yanked out some hair during a fight when we were kids. She might look sweet and all, with that quiet librarian thing she has going, but she can fight dirty, even when you're bigger than she is."

He had to laugh. He glanced over at Celeste, who was holding an upset preschooler on her lap and trying to calm him, her face close to his. Flynn did his best to imagine her in a physical fight with one of her sisters. He couldn't quite make the image fit, but had to admit he enjoyed trying.

She must have felt his gaze. She looked up from the little boy and whatever she was saying to him. He saw her swallow and watched her features turn rosy, much to his secret enjoyment. After a moment, she turned back to the child and he shifted his gaze back to Hope, who was watching him with interest.

"Looks as if we're just about wrapping up here," she said casually. "If you haven't had dinner, why don't you and your daughter come up to the ranch house after practice? Aunt Mary is making lasagna and her famous crusty bread sticks. You can celebrate with us."

"What are you celebrating?"

"We just agreed to let a film studio begin work on an animated Sparkle movie. It's going into production immediately, with hopes that it will be out by next Christmas. And with the money we're getting for the film rights, we're paying off the second mortgage our uncle took on the Star N. We'd love to have you celebrate with us."

His stomach rumbled on cue while he was still trying to take in the surprising invitation. "That's very kind of you, but I don't want to intrude."

"Intrude on what?" Another woman who looked enough like Celeste and Hope to make him certain this was their other sister joined them by the fireplace.

"I invited Flynn and his daughter over for lasagna. Aunt Mary won't mind, will she?"

"Are you kidding? She'll be over the moon to have a few more people to fuss over, and you know she always makes enough to feed half the town."

His first inclination was to say no. He even opened his mouth to refuse the invitation, but then he caught sight of Olivia looking more relaxed and animated than he had seen her in a long time. Right next to her was Celeste, apparently done calming the upset little boy and now smiling at something Olivia had said.

He couldn't seem to look away.

"Sure," he answered before he had a chance to think it through. He had no plans for dinner beyond warming up the pizza they'd had the night before, and he had a feeling Olivia was getting a little tired of his meager culinary abilities. "Thank you for inviting us. Lasagna sounds delicious, and we would be honored to celebrate with you, especially since Olivia is your biggest fan."

"Excellent," Hope said, looking delighted.

"I'd better call Aunt Mary and let her know to set two more places at dinner," Faith said.

The two of them walked away, leaving him wondering what he had just done.

Chapter Eight

This was a mistake.

Flynn sat at the big scarred kitchen table at the Star N wondering what on earth he had been thinking to agree to this.

Since the moment he sat down he had been aware of an itch between his shoulders, a feeling that he didn't belong here.

He couldn't quite put his finger on why.

The food was delicious, he had to admit. The lasagna was perfectly cooked, cheesy and flavorful with a red sauce his late mother's Italian chef would definitely have endorsed. The bread sticks were crispy and flavorful, and even the tossed salad seemed fresh and festive.

He couldn't fault the company. It was more than pleasant. He enjoyed listening to Celeste's family—her aunt Mary, who turned out to be a jolly woman with warm eyes and an ample girth, her two sisters as well as Hope's husband, Rafe Santiago, and Chase Brannon, a neighboring rancher who seemed more like part of the family.

More important, Olivia seemed to be more relaxed and comfortable than he had seen her in a long time. She sat at one end of the table with Celeste's niece, Louisa, her nephew, Barrett, and the other boy he had seen them with at the rehearsal. It turned out the boy was Rafe's nephew. From what Flynn could tell, the boy lived with Rafe and Hope, though Flynn didn't completely understand why.

The children were deep in conversation, and every once in a while he heard laughter coming from that end of the table. Olivia even joined in a few times—a total shocker.

So why did he feel so uneasy? He didn't want to admit that it might have been because he was enjoying himself *too* much. He didn't need to find more things that drew him to Celeste, when he already couldn't seem to get the woman out of his head.

"So what do you do in California?" Chase asked.

The man treated all the Nichols sisters as if he were an older brother. He seemed especially protective of Faith, though she hardly seemed to notice.

"Construction. I've got a fairly good-size operation, with offices in San Diego, Los Angeles and Sacramento."

"Delaney Construction. Is that you?" Rafe piped up.

He nodded, intensely proud of what he had built out of nothing. The company had become a powerhouse over the past decade, even in the midst of a rough economy.

"You do good work," Rafe said. "A buddy of mine is one of your carpentry subs. Kevin O'Brian. I flew out for a few weeks last spring to help him on a job, a new hospital in Fullerton."

"Right. He's a good man."

"That's what he said about you."

"Wow. Small world," Hope said.

He and the men spent a few moments talking about some of the unique challenges of working in the construction industry in Southern California.

"Have you ever thought about moving your operations out to this neck of the woods?" Chase asked. "We don't have a lot of hospitals and the like going up, but there are always construction projects around here, especially in the Jackson area."

The question took him by surprise. Three months ago he would have given an emphatic no to that question. He had a business in Southern California, contacts and sub-contractors and jobs he had fought hard to win.

He glanced at Olivia. He had other things to concern himself with now, like what might be best for his daughter.

Small-town life seemed to agree with her, he had to admit. Maybe she would be able to heal better if she were away for longer than just a few weeks from the life they had both known in California.

A change of scenery appeared to have helped the Nichols sisters move beyond the trauma in their past.

"I haven't," he answered truthfully. "It's definitely something to think about."

He glanced across the table to see Celeste listening in, though she was pretending not to.

What would she think if he stuck around town a little longer than a few weeks?

Probably nothing, he told himself. They meant nothing to each other.

"What are you doing with that property of your grand-mother's?" Mary asked.

"I'm hoping to put it up for sale in the next few weeks."

"You're not planning to subdivide it, are you?" she asked, her gaze narrowed.

He could probably make more money if he did that, but somehow he didn't think his grandparents would approve.

"That's a nice piece of land there by the Cold Creek," Brannon said. "Somebody could build a beautiful house on it if they were so inclined."

If he were going to stay here—which he most definitely *wasn't*, based on a simple dinner conversation—he probably would take the bones of the house and add on to it, opening up a wall here or there and rebuilding the kitchen and bathrooms.

It was a nice, comfortable house, perfectly situated with a gorgeous view of the mountains, but it was too small and cramped for comfort, with tiny rooms and an odd flow.

All this was theoretical. He planned to sell the property as-is, not take on another project. He had enough to do right now while he was helping his daughter recover the shattered bits of her life and learn to go on without the mother she had adored.

The conversation drifted during the dinner from topic to topic. The Nicholses seemed an eclectic group, with wide-ranging interests and opinions. Even the children joined in the discussion, discussing their projects at school, the upcoming show, the movie deal they were celebrating.

He was astonished to discover he enjoyed every moment of it. This was exactly what a family should be, he thought, noisy and chaotic and wonderful.

He had never known this growing up as an only child whose parents had stayed together much longer than they should have. He had learned to live without a family over the years, but it made his chest ache that his daughter would never have it, either.

Her sisters were matchmaking.

Celeste could tell by the surreptitious glances Faith and Hope sent between her and Flynn, the leading little questions they asked him, the way they not-so-subtly discussed the upcoming movie deal, careful to focus on Celeste's literary success, as if they were trying to sell a prize pig at the market.

It was humiliating, and she could only hope he hadn't noticed.

How could they possibly think Flynn might be interested in her in the first place? If they had bothered to ask her, she would have explained how ludicrous she found the very idea.

They didn't ask her, of course. They'd simply gone ahead and invited the poor man to dinner. Why he agreed to come, she had no idea. By the time dessert rolled around, she still hadn't figured it out—nor did she understand how he and Olivia seemed to fit in so effortlessly with her family.

Hope and Faith and Aunt Mary all liked him, she could tell, and Chase and Rafe treated him with courtesy and respect.

As for her, she liked having the two of them here entirely too much.

She tried to reel herself back, to force herself to remember this was only temporary. They were only at the ranch for the evening. Her sisters' matchmaking intentions were destined to failure. Not only *wasn't* he interested in her, but he had made it abundantly clear he was going back to California as soon as he could.

"Practice went well, don't you think?" Hope asked, distracting her from that depressing thought. "The kids seemed to be into it, and what I heard was wonderful."

"It won't win any Tony Awards, but it should be fun," she answered.

"With all you have going on around here, I still can't figure out why you decided to throw a show for local senior citizens," Flynn said.

Hope took the chance to answer him. "We've always had so much community support over the years here at The Christmas Ranch, from the very moment Uncle Claude opened the doors. The people of Pine Gulch have been great to us, and we wanted to give back a little. I guess we picked senior citizens because so many of them feel alone during the holiday season."

"Many of these people have been friends with me and my late husband for years," Mary added. "This seemed a good chance to offer them a little holiday spirit."

"I think it's nice," Louisa declared. "So do my friends. That's why they agreed to do it."

Celeste smiled at her niece, who had a very tender heart despite the tragedy of losing her father.

"I do, too," she answered.

"Is Sparkle going to show up at the party?" Barrett asked.

"I think we're going to have to see about that next week," Faith answered her son. "He's been acting a little down the past few days."

Celeste frowned at her sister. "What's wrong with him?" she asked, alarmed.

"Oh, I'm sure it's nothing," she answered. "He's just off his feed a bit. I ended up bringing him up here to his stall at the main barn to see if being back with the horses for a day or two would cheer him up."

Sparkle had a particularly soft spot for Mistletoe, an old mare who used to be Uncle Claude's. "I'm sure that's it," Celeste said.

"Maybe he just misses *you*, CeCe," Hope suggested. "You haven't been down to see him in a while."

Celeste rolled her eyes. "Right. I'm sure he's pining away."

It was true that she and Sparkle were old friends. The reindeer was warm and affectionate, far more than most of their small herd.

"You ought to go down to the barn to say hello while you're here," Faith suggested.

"Can I go meet Sparkle?" Olivia asked, her eyes huge as she followed the conversation. "I would *love* to."

She *had* told the girl she would take her to meet the inspiration for the books she loved so much. "He enjoys company. I'm sure he would love to meet you."

"Can we go now?" the girl pressed.

She looked at the table laden with delicious dishes she had done nothing to help prepare. Yes, she could claim a good excuse—being busy directing the show and all— but Uncle Claude and Aunt Mary had always been clear. If you didn't help cook a meal, you were obligated to help clean it up.

"I need to help clear these dishes first," she said.

"Oh, don't worry about this," Faith said.

"Right. We can take care of things," Hope insisted.

"Yes, dear," Aunt Mary added. "We've got this completely covered. It won't take a moment to clean this up.

Meantime, why don't you take our guests down to the barn to meet Sparkle?"

Who were these women and what had they done with her family members? She frowned, fighting the urge to roll her eyes at all of them for their transparent attempts to push her together with Flynn. For heaven's sake, what did they think would possibly happen between the two of them with his daughter along?

"I don't know," Flynn said, checking his watch. "It's getting late."

"It's not even eight o'clock yet!" Olivia protested. "Since I don't have to get up for school, I haven't been going to bed until nine thirty."

"I suppose that's true."

"So we can go?"

He hesitated, then shrugged. "If Celeste doesn't mind taking us. But we can't stay long. She's already had a long day."

"Oh, yay!" Olivia jumped up instantly from the table and headed for her coat.

"Does anyone else want to go down to the barn with us?" Celeste asked.

She didn't miss the way Barrett practically jumped out of his chair with eagerness but subsided again with a dejected look when his mother shook her head firmly.

Oh, she hoped Flynn hadn't noticed her crazy, delusional, interfering sisters.

He rose. "We'll probably need to head out after we stop at the barn. It's late and I have to get this young lady home to bed, whatever she says."

"Understandable," Aunt Mary said with a warm, affectionate smile for both of them.

With a sweet, surprising charm, he leaned in and

kissed her aunt's plump cheek. "Thank you for the delicious meal. We both truly enjoyed it."

She heard a definite ring of truth to his words, even as he looked a little surprised by them. She had the feeling he hadn't expected to enjoy the meal—which again made her wonder why he had agreed to come.

"You are most welcome," Aunt Mary said. "I hope both of you will come again before you return to California. Your grandmother was a dear, dear friend, and I miss her terribly. Having you and your daughter here helps ease that ache a little."

He looked touched. "I miss her, too. I only wish I could have visited her more the past few years."

Mary patted his hand. "She told me you called her every Sunday night without fail, and sometimes during the week, too. She was very proud of that fact, especially as so many young people these days get so busy with their lives that they forget that their parents and grandparents might be a touch lonely without them."

"A phone call was nothing. I can't tell you how much I appreciate all of her friends here in Pine Gulch who helped keep her busy and involved."

Celeste liked to consider herself one of that number. Charlotte had volunteered at the library almost up to the end of her life, never letting her physical ailments or the frailties of age prevent her from smiling and trying to lift someone else.

"She was always so proud of you," Mary went on. "Especially because of what you came from."

He gave a snort at that. "What I came from? Beverly Hills? Yeah. I overcame so much in life. I don't know why nobody has come out with a made-for-television movie about my sad life."

Mary made a face. "Charlotte was proud of many things about you, but perhaps most of all that despite every advantage you had, you always stayed grounded and didn't let your head get turned by your mother's fame or fortune. Now that I've met you, I understand what she meant. You're a good boy, Flynn Delaney."

She smiled and patted his hand again. Flynn looked a bit taken aback at anyone calling him a boy, but he only had time to give Aunt Mary a bemused sort of look before Olivia cut off anything he might have said in response.

"Are you ready, Daddy? I can't wait to see Sparkle. I can't *wait*."

"Yes. I'm ready. We can grab our coats on the way out. Thank you all again."

"You're so welcome," Faith and Hope said at the same time, almost as if they had rehearsed it. Chase and Rafe both nodded in the odd way men had of speaking volumes with just a simple head movement.

"Bye, Olivia. We'll see you at the next practice," Louisa said cheerfully.

They put on their coats quickly and headed out into the December evening.

The snow had increased in intensity, still light but more steady now. The air was still, though, with no wind to hurl flakes against them.

The night seemed magical somehow, hushed and beautiful with the full moon trying to push through the cloud cover.

Celeste was fiercely aware of him as they made their way to the barn. He was so very…male, from the jut of his jaw to his wide shoulders to the large footsteps his boots made in the snow beside her much smaller ones. He made her feel small and feminine in comparison.

To her relief, she didn't have to make conversation. Olivia kept up a steady stream of conversation about the ranch. She couldn't help noticing the girl had talked more that day than she had in all their previous encounters combined. Either she was more comfortable with Celeste now, or she was beginning to return to the girl she had been before the shooting.

If she wasn't mistaken, the girl had hardly limped that afternoon or evening. That had to be a good sign, she supposed.

"Here we are," she said when they reached the barn. The smell of hay and animals and old wood greeted them, not at all unappealing in its way.

She flipped on the lights and heard Mistletoe's distinctive whinny of greeting. She took time as they passed the old horse to give Misty a few strokes and an apple she pulled from her pocket before she led them to Sparkle's stall next door.

"Olivia, this is Sparkle. Sparkle, meet my good friend Olivia."

After a moment of coyness, the reindeer headed to the railing of the stall.

"I've never seen a real reindeer before. He's small!"

"Reindeer are generally much smaller than people think they should be." She petted him, much the way she had Mistletoe. He lipped at her, trying to find a treat.

"Would you like to feed him an apple?"

"Can I?"

She glanced down at the girl and decided not to miss this opportunity. "I don't know. You'll have to use your left arm. He prefers it when people feed him from that side."

That was an out-and-out lie. Sparkle would eat with

great delight any apple that came his way, but she decided Olivia didn't need to know that.

Flynn made a low sound of amusement beside her that seemed to ripple down her spine. She barely managed to hold back her instinctive shiver as she handed the apple to Olivia.

The girl narrowed her gaze at Celeste, obviously trying to figure out if this was some kind of a trick. In the end, the appeal and novelty of feeding a reindeer outweighed her suspicions.

She took the apple with her injured left hand and, with effort, held it out to the reindeer, who nibbled it out of her hand. Olivia giggled. "Can I pet him?"

"Sure. He won't hurt you."

She rubbed his head for a moment. "What about his antlers?"

"Go ahead. Just be gentle."

She reached out and tentatively touched an antler. "It's hard and soft at the same time. Weird!"

Sparkle visited with her for a moment, and it was plain he was happy to find a new friend. Any malaise the reindeer might have been feeling was nowhere in evidence. Maybe he really *had* been pining for her, but she doubted it. Maybe, like the rest of them, he just needed a little break from the hectic pace of the holiday season.

"What's special about this particular reindeer?" Flynn asked.

She considered how to answer. "Well, he was the first reindeer Uncle Claude ever obtained, so he's been here the longest. And he's always been so much more affectionate than the others—not that they're mean or anything, just…standoffish. Not Sparkle. He's always been as friendly as can be. It rubs off on everyone."

They watched the reindeer a few moments longer. When she heard a little sound from the stall at the end of the barn, she suddenly remembered what other treasure the barn contained. Clearly, she didn't spend enough time here.

"I nearly forgot," she said. "There's something else here you might like to see."

"What?" Olivia asked eagerly. The girl loved animals; that much was obvious. Perhaps she and Flynn ought to look into getting a dog when they returned to California.

She didn't want to think about that now, not when the night seemed hushed and sweet here in the quiet barn.

"Come and see," she answered. She led the way and pulled open the stall gate. Olivia peered in a little warily but her nervousness gave way to excitement.

"Puppies! Dad, look!"

"I see them, honey."

The half dozen black-and-white pudgy things belonged to Georgie, one of the ranch border collies.

"Can I pet them?"

"Sure. I'll warn you, they're probably not super clean. You're going to want to wash your hands when you're done."

"I will. I promise."

She knelt down and was immediately bombarded with wriggling puppies.

Celeste felt her throat tighten as she watched this girl who had been through so much find simple joy in the moment. Flynn had almost lost her. It seemed a miracle that they were here in this barn on a snowy night watching her giggle as a puppy licked her hand.

"She did all right today at the rehearsal," she said in a low voice to Flynn as they watched together. "I know you were concerned about the noise and confusion, but she handled it well. Wouldn't you agree?"

They were standing close enough together that she could feel his sigh. "I suppose."

"Does that mean you'll bring her to the next rehearsal, then?"

He gave a small sound that was almost a laugh. "Anybody ever tell you that you're relentless?"

"A few times, maybe," she said ruefully. *More than a few* was closer to the truth.

Needing a little distance, she eased down onto the bench next to the stall. To her surprise, he followed and sat beside her.

"Fine," he answered. "You win. I'll bring her to the next one. That doesn't mean I have to like it."

She glanced at his daughter playing with the puppies a dozen feet away, then turned back to Flynn. "Why do you have a problem with her performing?" she asked, her voice low. "Especially when it seems to be something she enjoys?"

"I don't *want* her to enjoy it," he answered in an equally low tone. "If I had my way, I would have her stay far away from any kind of stage or screen."

She frowned at the intensity of his words. "Because of your mother or because of Elise?"

"Either. Both. Take your pick." He watched as a puppy started nibbling on Olivia's ponytail, which only made her giggle again as she tried to extricate it from the little mouth.

After a moment he spoke with fierce resolve. "I want my daughter to find happiness in life based on her own decisions and accomplishments, not because of how many pictures of her holding a latte from Starbucks showed up in the tabloids this week. There's an artificiality to that world that crumbles to nothing in a heartbeat. Take it from someone who grew up on the edge of that spotlight."

She thought of what Aunt Mary had said about his grandmother's pride in him for staying grounded. Unlike his mother or his wife, he hadn't sought that spotlight. He had gone into a career outside Hollywood and had built a successful business on his own merits. She had to admire that.

"That must have been tough for you," she said.

He shrugged. "How can I complain, really? It sounds stupid, even to me. I grew up with the sort of privileges most people only dream about. A-list celebrities hanging out in my swimming pool, a BMW in the driveway on my sixteenth birthday, vacations in Cannes and Park City and Venice."

By worldly standards, her family had been very poor. Her parents had given everything they had to helping others, to the point that she remembered a period in their lives when she and her sisters each had had only two or three outfits that they swapped back and forth.

She hadn't necessarily enjoyed moving from country to country, never feeling as if she had a stable home. In truth, she still carried lingering resentment about it, but she had always known she was deeply loved.

She had a feeling that for all his outward privilege, Flynn had missed out on that assurance, at least from his parents. She was grateful he had known the unwavering love and devotion of his grandmother.

"We don't get to choose the circumstances of our birth families, do we?" she said softly. "The only thing we have control of is the life we make for ourselves out of those circumstances."

His gaze met hers and the intensity of his expression left her suddenly breathless. Something shimmered between them, something bright and fierce. She couldn't seem to look away, and she again had the oddest feeling he wanted to kiss her.

Now? Here? With his daughter just a few feet away? She must have been imagining things. Still, the idea of him leaning forward slightly, of his mouth sliding across hers, made nerves jump in her stomach and her knees feel suddenly weak.

She felt as if she stood on the brink of something, arms stretched wide, trying to find the courage to jump into the empty space beyond.

She could lose her heart so easily to this man.

The thought whispered into her mind and she swallowed hard. With the slightest of nudges, she would leap into that empty space and doubtless crash hard back to earth.

Careful, she warned herself, and looked away from him, pretending to focus on his daughter and the cute, wriggling puppies.

After a long pause, he finally spoke. "Despite everything you and your sisters have been through, you've made a good life for yourself here in Pine Gulch."

"I'd like to think so." Okay, maybe she was a little lonely. Maybe there were nights she lay in bed and stared at the ceiling, wondering if she was destined to spend the rest of her nights alone.

"I guess you know a little about being in the spotlight now, don't you?" Flynn said.

She forced a little laugh. "Not really. My particular spotlight is more like a flashlight beam. A very tiny, focused flashlight. That's the nice thing about being only a name on a book cover."

"That will change when the Sparkle movie hits the big screen," he predicted.

Oh, she didn't want to think about that. Just the idea made her feel clammy and slightly queasy. "I hope not," she said fervently. "I like being under the radar."

He frowned. "Why agree to let someone make the movie, then? You had to know that's only going to increase your celebrity status. You won't be able to stay under the radar for long."

In her heart, she knew he was right. What had she gotten herself into?

She hadn't had a choice, she reminded herself. Not really.

"I love my family," she said. "They're everything to me."

"It only took me a few minutes at dinner tonight to figure that out. You have a great family. But what does that have to do with signing a movie deal you don't appear to want?"

For someone who loved the magic and power in words, sometimes in conversation she felt as if she never could manage to find the right ones.

"Things haven't been…easy around here the past few years, even before my brother-in-law's accident. My uncle was a wonderful man but not the best businessman around, and the ranch hasn't exactly been thriving financially."

"I'm sorry to hear that."

"The, um, increased interest in The Christmas Ranch after the first Sparkle book came out last season helped a great deal but didn't completely solve the cash flow woes." She felt her face heat a little, as it always did when she talked about the astonishing success of the book. "With the deal Hope and I will be signing for the movie rights, we can pay off the rest of the ranch's debts and push the operation firmly into the black, which will lift considerable pressure from Faith. How could I turn down something that will benefit my family so much?"

He studied her for a moment, that funny intensity in his expression again. "So it's not necessarily what you really want, but you're willing to go through with it anyway for your family."

"Something like that," she muttered.

"If having a movie made out of your book doesn't sit well with you, couldn't you have found an alternative revenue stream?"

She shrugged. "Hope and I talked at length about this. Our agent and publisher were clear. *Someone* was going to make a Sparkle movie—which, believe me, is an amazing position to find ourselves in. The terms of this particular deal were very favorable for Hope and for me, and we were both impressed by the other projects this particular production company has engineered. The moment seemed right."

"I'm *glad* they're making a Sparkle movie," Olivia said suddenly. Celeste had been so busy explaining herself, she hadn't realized the girl had left the puppies on the floor of the stall and rejoined them. "I can't wait to see it."

Flynn smiled at his daughter with that sweet tenderness that tugged at her heart. "We'll probably be back in California, and you can tell everyone else at the movie theater that you actually had the chance to meet the real Sparkle and the women who created the fictional version."

"I guess." Olivia didn't look as excited about that prospect as Celeste might have expected. In fact, she appeared downright glum.

Why? she wondered. Was the girl enjoying her time in Pine Gulch so much that she didn't like thinking about their eventual return to California?

"Maybe we could come back and see the movie here," Olivia suggested.

"Maybe."

Celeste felt a sharp little kick to her heart at the non-committal word. They wouldn't be back. She was suddenly certain of it. After Flynn sold his grandmother's house, he would have no more ties here in Pine Gulch. She likely would never see him or his daughter again.

This was why she needed to be careful to guard her heart better. She already hurt just thinking about them leaving. How much worse would it be if she let herself take that leap and fell in love with him?

He stood up and wiped the straw from the back of Olivia's coat where she had been sitting on the floor of the stall.

"We should probably take off," he said. "You need to tell Celeste thank-you for bringing you out here to meet Sparkle and to play with the puppies."

"Do we have to go?" she complained.

"Yes. It's late and Celeste probably has to work at the library tomorrow."

She nodded and was suddenly overwhelmed by a wave of fatigue. The day had been long and exhausting, and right now she wanted nothing more than to be in her comfy clothes, cuddled up with her animals and watching something brainless on TV.

"Okay," Olivia said in a dejected voice. "Thank you

for bringing me down here to meet Sparkle and play with the puppies."

"You are very welcome," Celeste said. "Anytime you want to come back, we would love to have you. Sparkle would, too."

Olivia seemed heartened by that as she headed for the reindeer's stall one last time.

"Bye, Sparkle. Bye!"

The reindeer nodded his head two or three times as if he was bowing, which made the girl giggle.

Celeste led the way out of the barn. Another inch of snow had fallen during the short time they had been inside, and they walked in silence to where his SUV was parked in front of the house.

She wrapped her coat around her while Flynn helped his daughter into the backseat. Once she was settled, he closed the door and turned to her.

"Please tell your family thank you for inviting me to dinner. I enjoyed it very much."

"I will. Good night."

With a wave, he hopped into his SUV and backed out of the driveway.

She watched them for just a moment, snow settling on her hair and her cheeks while she tried to ignore that little ache in her heart.

She could do this. She was tougher than she sometimes gave herself credit for being. Yes, she might already care about Olivia and be right on the brink of falling hard for her father. That didn't mean she had to lean forward and leave solid ground.

She would simply have to keep herself centered, focused on her family and her friends, her work and her writing and the holidays. She would do her best to keep him at arm's length. It was the only smart choice if she wanted to emerge unscathed after this holiday season.

Soon they would be gone and her life would return to the comfortable routine she had created for herself.

As she walked into the house, she tried not to think about how unappealing she suddenly found that idea.

Chapter Nine

She didn't have a chance to test her resolve, simply because she didn't see Flynn again for longer than a moment or two over the next few days.

At the Thursday rehearsal, he merely dropped Olivia off and left after making sure to give Hope—not Celeste—a card with his cell phone number on it.

She supposed she should take that as some sort of progress. From what she gathered, he hadn't let Olivia out of his sight since the accident. She had to feel good that he felt comfortable enough with her and her family to leave the girl at The Christmas Ranch without him.

On the other hand, she had to wonder if maybe he was just trying to avoid her.

That really made no logical sense. Why would he feel any sort of need to avoid her? *He* wasn't the one who was developing feelings that could never go anywhere.

Still, she had to wonder, especially when he did the same thing Saturday morning for their final practice before the performance, just dropping Olivia off as most of the other parents had done.

She should be grateful he'd brought the girl at all, especially when he obviously wasn't thrilled about the whole thing.

It was too bad, really, because Olivia was a natural in front of an audience. She seemed far more comfortable onstage than the other children.

The performance was nothing elaborate, a rather hodgepodge collection of short Christmas skits mixed with songs and poems, but considering the few practices they'd had, the show came together marvelously.

When they finished the second run-through Saturday morning, Celeste clapped her hands.

"That was amazing!" she exclaimed. "I'm so proud of each one of you for all your hard work. You are going to make some people very, very happy next week."

Jolie Wheeler raised her hand. "Can we take the costumes home to show our moms and dads?"

None of the costumes was anything fancy, just bits and pieces she and Hope had thrown together with a little help from Faith and a few of the parents. "We need to keep them here so we can make sure everyone has all the pieces—the belts and halos and crowns—they need for the performance. When you take them off, put your costume on the hanger and everything else in the bag with your name on it in the dressing room. Remember, you will all have to be here at five thirty sharp so we can get into costume and be ready for the show. We'll have the performance first, and then you are all welcome with your families to stay for dinner with our guests, if you'd like. There should be plenty of food for everyone."

"Then can we take the costumes home?" Jolie asked.

She smiled at the adorable girl. "We need to keep them here just in case we decide to do another show at The Christmas Ranch next year."

"Rats," Jolie complained and a few others joined her in grumbling. What they wanted to do with a few hokey costumes, Celeste had no idea, but she had to smile at their disappointment.

"You'll all just have to be in the show next year so you can wear them again," she said.

Not that she intended to be part of it, even if Hope begged her. Writing the little show had taken her almost as long as a full-fledged children's book.

"Thank you all again for your hard work, and I'll see you Tuesday evening at five thirty if you need help with your hair and makeup."

The children dispersed to the boys' and girls' dressing rooms—really just separate storage spaces that had been temporarily converted for the show. She cleaned up the rehearsal space and supervised the pickup of the children.

Finally, only Louisa, Barrett, Joey and Olivia were left. They didn't seem to mind. Indeed, they had gone to the game drawer Hope kept in her office to keep the children occupied when they were hanging out at the lodge and were playing a spirited game of Go Fish with a Christmas-themed deck of cards.

Though she had a hundred things to—including finishing the paint job on the backdrop for the little stage they had rigged up—she sat down at the table near the refreshment booth where they were playing.

"You did so well today. All of you."

"Thanks," Louisa said. "It's really fun. I hope we do it again next year."

Not unless Hope found some other sucker to be in charge, she thought again.

"I've had lots of fun, too," Olivia said. "Thanks for inviting me to do it."

"You're very welcome. How are things going at your great-grandmother's house?"

As soon as she asked the question, she wished she hadn't. It sounded entirely too much as if she was snooping. She might as well have come out and asked when they were leaving.

"Good, I guess. We have two more rooms to do. My dad said we'll probably go back to California between Christmas and New Year's."

She tried to ignore the sharp pang in her chest. "I'm sure you'll be glad to be back in your own house."

"You're lucky! You can go swimming in the ocean," Louisa said.

"Sometimes. Mostly, it's too cold, except in summer."

"And you can go to Disneyland whenever you want," Joey added.

"No, I can't," she protested. "I have to go to school and stuff."

They talked more about the differences between their respective homes. Olivia was quite envious that they could ride horses and go sledding all winter long while the other children thought California was only palm trees and beaches.

While the seasonal staff of The Christmas Ranch started arriving and getting ready for the busiest day of their season, the children continued their game, and Celeste sat at the table next to them working on a drawing for a complicated part of the stage she was hoping Rafe could help her finish later that day.

Finally, about forty-five minutes after practice ended, Flynn burst through the front doors looking harried. "Sorry I'm late. I was taking a load of things to the county landfill and it took longer than I expected."

"Don't even worry about it. The kids have been enjoying themselves. Haven't you?"

"Yep," Barrett said. "'Cause I won Go Fish three times and Joey and Olivia both won once. Louisa didn't win any."

"Next time, watch out," his sister declared.

Flynn smiled at the girl, that full-fledged charming smile Celeste remembered from when he was a teenager. She had to swallow hard and force herself to look away, wondering why it suddenly felt so warm in the lodge.

"How was practice?" he asked.

"Good," she answered. "Great, actually. Everyone worked so hard."

"I can't wait for you to see the show, Dad," Olivia declared. "It's going to be *so* good. Celeste says all the ladies will cry."

He looked vaguely alarmed. "Is that right? Will I cry, too? I'd better bring a big hankie, just in case."

She giggled hard, then in the funny way kids have, she looked at Barrett and Louisa and something in their expressions made her laugh even harder, until all three were busting up. Their laughter was infectious and Celeste couldn't help smiling.

Flynn gazed at the three children, certain he was witnessing a miracle.

This was really his daughter, looking bright and animated and...happy.

This was the daughter he remembered, this girl who found humor in the silliest things, who was curious about the world around her and loved talking with people. He'd feared she was gone forever, stolen by a troubled man who had taken so much else from her.

Seeing her sitting at a table in the St. Nicholas Lodge, laughing with Celeste and her niece and nephew, he wanted to hug all three of the children. Even more, he wanted to kiss Celeste right on that delicious-looking mouth of hers that had haunted his dreams for days.

Her smiling gaze met his and a wave of tenderness washed over him. She had done this. He didn't know how. She had seen a sad, wounded girl and had worked some kind of Sparkle magic on her to coax out the sweet and loving girl Olivia used to be.

Her smile slid away and he realized he was staring. He drew in a deep breath and forced himself to look away.

His gaze landed on a piece of paper with what looked like a complicated drawing. "I didn't know you were an artist."

She looked embarrassed. "I'm *so* not an artist, Hope is. I'm just trying to work up a sketch I can show Rafe. I'm trying to figure out how to build wings on the side of the stage so the children have somewhere to wait off-stage. There's no time to sew curtains. I just need some sort of screen to hide them from view.

He studied her sketch, then took the paper from her and made a few quick changes. "That shouldn't be hard," he said. "You just have to build a frame out of two-by-fours and then use something lightweight like particle board for your screen. If it's hinged and connected there, it should be solid and also portable enough that you can store it somewhere when you're not using it."

She studied the drawing. "Wow. That's genius! You know, I think that just might work. Can you just write down what supplies you think it might need? Rafe will be back from Jackson Hole shortly, and I can put him to work on it if he has time."

He glanced at the stage, then at his daughter, still smiling as she played cards with the other two children. Though he knew he would probably regret it—and he certainly had plenty of things still to take care of at Charlotte's house—he spoke quickly before he could change his mind.

"If you've got some tools I can use and the two-by-fours, I can probably get the frame for it done in no time."

She stared at him, green eyes wide behind those sexy glasses she wore. "Seriously?"

He shrugged. "I started out in carpentry. It's kind of what I do. This shouldn't be hard at all—as long as Olivia doesn't mind hanging around a little longer."

"Yay!" Louisa exclaimed. "She can come to the house and decorate the sugar cookies we made last night with Aunt Celeste while our mom was Christmas shopping."

Olivia looked suitably intrigued. "I've never decorated sugar cookies."

"Never?" Celeste exclaimed. She looked surprised enough that Flynn felt a pinch of guilt. Apparently this was another area where he had failed his daughter.

Olivia shook her head. "Is it hard?"

"No way," Louisa answered. "It's easy and super, super fun. You can decorate the cookies any way you want. There's no right or wrong. You can use sparkly sugar or M&M's or frosting or whatever you want."

"The best part is, when you mess it up, you get to eat

your mistakes," Barrett added. "Nobody even cares. I mess up a *lot*."

Olivia snickered and Flynn had a feeling *she* would be messing up plenty, too. What was it with all these Christmas traditions that filled kids with more sugar when they least needed another reason to be excited?

He had struck out miserably when it came to Christmas traditions this year. At least they had the little Christmas tree at his grandmother's house for decoration, but that was about it.

Olivia had insisted she hoped Santa Claus wouldn't come that year, but he had disregarded her wishes and bought several things online for her. A few other presents would be waiting back in California, sort of a delayed holiday, simply because the new bike her physical therapist suggested was too big for the journey here in his SUV.

Next year would be different, he told himself. By this time next year they would be established in a routine back in California. They could hang stockings and put up a tree of their own and decorate all the sugar cookies she wanted, even if he had to order ready-made plain cookies from his favorite bakery.

The idea of returning to a routine after the stress of the past few months should have been appealing. Instead, it left him remarkably unenthused.

"May I go, Dad? I really, really, *really* want to decorate cookies."

He was torn between his desire to keep her close and his deep relief that she was so obviously enjoying the company of other children. She would enjoy the cookie decorating far more than she would enjoy sitting around and watching him work a band saw.

"Are you sure your aunt won't mind one more?" he asked Celeste.

"Are you kidding? Mary loves a crowd. The more the merrier, as far as she's concerned." She smiled a little. "And look at it this way. You'll probably come out of the whole thing with cookies to take home."

"Well, in that case, how can I say no? A guy always needs a few more cookies."

"Yay! I can go," Olivia told the other children as if they hadn't been right there to hear her father's decision.

"Put the cards away first and then get your coats on. Then you can walk up to the house."

"You're not coming?" Olivia asked.

"I'll be up later," she answered with a smile. "But first I have to finish painting some of the scenery."

The children cleaned up the cards and returned them to a little tin box, then put on their coats, hats and mittens. As soon as they were on their way, Celeste turned to him with a grateful smile. She looked so fresh and lovely that for a crazy moment, he wished they were alone in the lodge with that big crackling fire.

Instead, an older woman was setting out prepackaged snacks in what looked like a concessions area and another one was arranging things on a shelf in a gift store. Outside the windows, he could see families beginning to queue up to buy tickets.

"Is there somewhere I can get going on this? A workshop or something?"

"Oh." She looked flustered suddenly and he wondered if something in his expression revealed the fierce attraction simmering through him. "Yes. There's a building behind back where Rafe keeps his tools. That's where I've been painting the scenery, too. I'll show you."

She led the way through the lodge to a back door. They walked through the pale winter sunshine to a modern-looking barn a short distance away.

In a pasture adjacent to the barn, he saw several more reindeer as well as some draft horses.

"This is where we keep the reindeer at night during the holiday season," she explained. "There's Sparkle. Do you see him?"

As far as he could tell all the reindeer looked the same, but he would take her word for it. "Is he feeling better?"

"Much. Apparently he only wanted a few days off."

"Olivia will be happy to hear that."

"He'll need his strength. This afternoon and evening will be crazy busy."

"For the reindeer, too?" he asked, fascinated by the whole idea of an entire operation devoted only to cele-brating the holidays.

"Yes. Hope will probably hook them up to the sleigh for photo ops and short rides. The draft horses, of course, will be taking people on sleigh rides around the ranch, which is a highlight of the season. You should take Olivia. She would love it. It's really fun riding through the cold, starry night all bundled up in blankets."

It did sound appealing—especially if he and Celeste were alone under those blankets...

He jerked his brain back to the business at hand. He really needed to stop this.

"We're only open a few more nights," she said. "But if you want to take her, let me know and I'll arrange it."

As much as he thought Olivia would enjoy the sleigh ride, he wasn't at all certain that spending more time at The Christmas Ranch with Celeste and her appealing family would be good for either of them.

"We'll see," he said, unwilling to commit to anything. "Shall we get to it?"

"Right. Of course."

She led him into a well-lit, modern building with stalls along one wall. The rest seemed to be taken up with storage and work space.

She led him to an open area set up with a band saw, a reciprocating saw, a router and various other power tools, as well as a stack of two-by-fours and sheets of plywood.

"You might not need to have Rafe run to the lumber yard. You might have everything here."

"Great."

She pointed to another area of the barn where other large pieces of plywood had been painted with snowflakes. "I need to finish just a few things on the scenery, so I'll be on hand if you need help with anything."

The best help she could offer would be to stay out of his way. She was entirely too tempting to his peace of mind, but he couldn't figure out a way to say that without sounding like an idiot, so he just decided to focus on the job at hand.

"Do you mind if I turn on some music?" she asked.

"That's fine," he answered. Her place, her music.

It wasn't Christmas music, he was happy to hear. Instead, she found some classic-rock station and soon The Eagles were harmonizing through the barn from a speaker system in the work area.

She returned to her side of the area and started opening paint cans and gathering brushes, humming along to the music. Though he knew he needed to get started, he couldn't seem to look away.

He liked watching her. She seemed to throw herself into everything she did, whether that was directing a ragtag group of children in a Christmas show, telling stories to a bunch of energetic school kids or writing a charming story about a brave reindeer.

He was fascinated with everything about her.

He had to get over it, he told himself sternly. He needed to help build her set, finish clearing out his grandmother's house and then go back to his normal life in California.

He turned his attention to the pile of lumber and found the boards he would need. Then he spent a moment familiarizing himself with another man's work space and the tools available to him. Rafe Santiago kept a clean, well-organized shop. He would give him that.

The moment he cut the first board, he felt more centered than he had in a long time. He was very good at building things. It gave him great satisfaction to take raw materials and turn them into something useful, whether that was a piece of furniture or a children's hospital.

For nearly an hour, they worked together in a comfortable silence broken only by the sounds of tools and the music. He made good progress by doing his best to pretend she wasn't there, that this growing attraction simmering through him would burn itself out when it no longer had the fuel of her presence to sustain it.

The barn was warmer than he would have expected, especially with the air compressor going to power the tools, and soon he was down to his T-shirt. Before she started painting, she had taken off the sweater she wore, but it wasn't until he took a break and looked up from connecting two boards that he saw the message on it: Wake up Smarter. Sleep With a Librarian.

For an instant his mind went completely blank as all the blood left his head at the image. Unfortunately, his finger twitched on the trigger of the unfamiliar nail gun, which was far more reactive than any of the guns he was used to.

He felt a sharp biting pain as the nail impaled the webbing between the forefinger and thumb of his left hand to the board. He swore and ripped out the nail, mortified at his stupidity.

It wasn't the first time he'd had an accident with a nail gun or a power tool—in his line of work, nobody made it through without nicks and bruises and a few stitches here or there, especially starting out—but it was completely embarrassing. He hadn't made that kind of rookie mistake in years. Apparently, she wasn't very good for his concentration.

"What happened?" she asked.

"Nothing. It's fine." It was, really. The nail hadn't gone through anything but skin.

"You're bleeding. Let me see."

"It's just a poke. Hazard of the job."

"I think Rafe keeps a first-aid kit somewhere in here." She started rifling through cabinets until she found one.

"I don't need anything. It's almost stopped bleeding."

It still burned like hell, but he wasn't about to tell her that.

"I'll feel better if you let me at least clean it up."

"Really, not necessary."

She ignored him and stepped closer, bringing that delicious springtime scent with her that made him think of sunlit mornings and new life.

"Hold out your hand."

Since he was pretty certain she wouldn't let up until he cooperated, he knew he had no choice but to comply. Feeling stupid, he thrust out his arm. She took his injured hand in both of hers and dabbed at it with a wipe she'd found inside the kit.

"It's not bad," she murmured. "I don't think you're going to need stitches."

He did his best to keep his gaze fiercely away from that soft T-shirt that had caused the trouble in the first place—and the curves beneath it.

The gentle touch of her fingers on his skin made him want to close his eyes and lean into her. It had been so long since he'd known that kind of aching sweetness.

She smiled a little. "Do you remember that time I fell on my bike in front of your grandmother's house?"

"Yes." His voice sounded a little ragged around the edges, but he had to hope she didn't notice.

"You were so sweet to me," she said with soft expression as she applied antiseptic cream to the tiny puncture wound. "I couldn't even manage to string two words together around you, but you just kept up a steady stream of conversation to make me feel more comfortable until my aunt Mary could come pick me up. I was so mortified, but you made it feel less horrible."

He swallowed. He'd done that? He didn't have much memory of it, only of a quiet girl with big eyes and long dark hair.

"Why would you be mortified? It was an accident."

She snorted a little. "Right. I ran into your grandmother's mailbox because I wasn't paying attention to where I was going. It was all your fault for mowing the lawn without your shirt on."

He stared down at her. "*That's* why you crashed?"

She looked up and he saw shadows of remembered embarrassment there. "In my defense, I was thirteen years old, you were a much older boy and I already had a huge crush on you. It's a wonder I could say a word."

"Is that right?" he asked softly. Her fingers felt so good on his skin, her luscious mouth was *right there* and he wanted nothing but to find a soft spot of hay somewhere for the two of them to collapse into.

"Yes," she murmured, and he saw answering awareness in her eyes. "And then you made it so much worse by being so kind, cleaning me up, calling my aunt, then fixing my bike for me. What shy, awkward bookworm alive could have resisted that, when the cutest boy she'd ever met in real life was so sweet to her?"

He didn't want to be sweet right now. At her words, hunger growled to life inside him, and he knew he would have to appease it somehow.

Just a kiss, he told himself. A simple taste and then they both could move on.

He lowered his mouth and felt her hands tremble when his lips brushed hers.

She tasted just as delicious as he would have imagined, sweet and warm and luscious, like nibbling at a perfectly ripe strawberry.

She froze for just a moment, long enough for him to wonder if he'd made a terrible error in judgment, and then her mouth softened and she kissed him back with a breathy sigh, as if she had been waiting for this since that day half a lifetime ago.

Her hands fluttered against his chest for just a moment, then wrapped around his neck, and he pulled her closer, delighting in her soft curves and the aching tenderness of the kiss.

Chapter Ten

Life could take the strangest turns sometimes.

If someone had told her a week ago that she would be standing in The Christmas Ranch barn on a Saturday afternoon kissing Flynn Delaney, she would have advised them to see somebody about their delusions.

Here they were, though, with her hands tangled in his hair and his arms wrapped around her and his mouth doing intoxicating things to her.

She wanted the moment to go on forever, this sultry, honeyed magic.

Nothing in her limited experience compared to this. She'd had a couple of boyfriends in college, nothing serious and nothing that had lasted more than a month or two—and absolutely nothing that prepared her for the sheer sensual assault of kissing Flynn.

She made a little sound in her throat and he deepened

the kiss, his tongue sliding along hers as his arms tightened around her. Sensation rippled through her, and she could only be grateful when he pushed her against the nearest cabinet, his mouth hot and demanding.

She couldn't seem to think about anything other than kissing him, touching him, finding some way to be closer to him. She wrapped her arms more tightly around his neck, wanting this moment to go on forever.

They kissed for a long time there with the scents of sawdust and hay swirling around them. Even as she lost herself in the kiss, some tiny corner of her brain was trying to catalog every emotion and sensation, storing it up so she could relive it after he was gone. The taste of him, of coffee and mint and sexy male, the silky softness of his hair, the delicious rasp of his whiskers against her skin, his big, warm hands slipping beneath the back of her T-shirt to slide against her bare skin…

"Celeste? Are you in here?"

She heard her brother-in-law's voice and felt as if he had just thrown her into the snow. Rafe and Hope must have returned earlier than they'd planned.

She froze and scrambled away from Flynn, yanking her T-shirt back down and trying frantically to catch her breath.

He was having the same trouble, she realized, as he quickly stepped behind one of the power tools to hide the evidence of his arousal.

Had *she* done that to him? She couldn't quite believe it.

"Celeste?" she heard again.

"In…" The words caught in her throat and she had to clear them away before she spoke again. "In here."

An instant later Rafe walked into the work space. He

stopped and gazed between the two of them and she saw his mouth tighten, a sudden watchful glint in his eyes.

Rafe was a tough man, extremely protective of each Nichols sister—probably because he had once saved all their lives. His sharp gaze took in the scene and she doubted he could miss her heightened color, her swollen lips, their heavy breathing.

She was sure of it when he aimed a hard, narrow-eyed look at Flynn.

She could feel herself flush more and then told herself she was being ridiculous, feeling like a teenager caught necking on the front porch by her older brother. She was a grown woman, twenty-eight years old, and she could kiss half the men in town if she wanted.

She'd just never wanted to before.

"Hope said you might need some help building a few things for the set."

"Flynn has been helping me."

"So I see," Rafe drawled.

"Thanks for letting me use your shop," Flynn said. "I tried to be careful with the tools, but your nail gun got away from me." He held up the hand she had bandaged.

"It's got a fast trigger. Sorry about that. Anything I can do to help you wrap things up so you can get out of here?"

"Another pair of hands never hurts," Flynn answered.

Celeste finally felt as if her brain cells were beginning to function again.

"I'm about done painting. I…think I'll just clean my brushes and leave you to it. I should probably head up to the house to help Aunt Mary with the cookie decorating."

She couldn't meet either of their gazes as she walked past the men, feeling like an idiot.

"Nice shirt," Rafe murmured in a low voice as she passed him.

Baffled, she glanced down and then could have died from mortification. It was the Sleep with a Librarian shirt that Hope and Faith had given her one Christmas as a joke. She never wore it, of course—it wasn't her style *at all*—but she'd thrown it on that morning under her sweater, knowing she was going to be painting the scenery later and it would be perfect for the job.

She gathered her brushes quickly and headed for the sink in the small bathroom of the barn.

While she cleaned the brushes, she glanced into the mirror and saw it was worse than she had thought. Her hair had come half out of the messy bun, her lips were definitely swollen and her cheeks were rosier than St. Nicholas's in "'Twas the Night Before Christmas."

Oh, she wanted to *die*. Rafe knew she had just been making out with Flynn, which meant he would definitely tell Hope. Her sisters would never let her hear the end of it.

That was the least of her problems, she realized.

Now that she had kissed the man and knew how amazing it was, how would she ever be able to endure not being able to do it again?

What just happened here?

Even after Celeste left to clean her brushes, Flynn could feel his heart hammering, his pulse racing.

Get a grip, he told himself. It was just a kiss. But for reasons he didn't completely understand, it somehow struck him as being so much more.

He couldn't seem to shake the feeling that something

momentous had occurred in that kiss, something terrifying and mysterious and tender.

Why had he kissed her?

The whole time they'd shared the work space, he had been telling himself all the reasons why he needed to stay away from her. At the first opportunity and excuse, he had ignored all his common sense and swooped right in.

What shy, awkward bookworm alive could have resisted that, when the cutest boy she'd ever met in real life was so sweet to her?

She'd once had a crush on him. He didn't know why that made him feel so tender toward the quiet girl she had been.

That kiss had rocked him to the core and left him feeling off balance, as if he'd just slipped on the sawdust and landed hard on his ass. For a moment, he closed his eyes, remembering those lush curves against him, her enthusiastic response, the soft, sexy little sounds she made.

"What are you doing here?" For one horrible moment he thought Rafe was calling him out for kissing Celeste, until he realized the other man was gazing down at the set piece he was building.

Focus, he told himself. Get the job done, as he'd promised.

"She wants some kind of wings on the side of the stage for the children to wait behind until it's their turn to go on," he explained. He went into detail about his plan and listened while Rafe made a few excellent suggestions to improve the design.

"This shouldn't take us long to finish up," the other man said. "In fact, I probably could handle it on my own, if you want to get out of here."

That sounded a little more strongly worded than just

a suggestion. "I'm good," he answered, a little defiantly. "I like to finish what I start."

He was aware as they went to work of her cleaning up her brushes, closing up the paint cans, putting her sweater back on to hide that unexpectedly enticing T-shirt.

He was also aware that she hadn't looked at him once since she'd jerked out of his arms when her brother-in-law had come in.

Was she regretting that they had kissed? He couldn't tell. She *should* regret it, since they both had to know it was a mistake, but somehow it still bothered him that she might.

Did he owe her some kind of apology for kissing her out of the blue like that? Something else he didn't know.

He had been faithful to his vows, as misguided as they had been, and his relationships since then had been with women who wanted the same thing he did: uncomplicated, no-strings affairs.

Celeste was very different from those women—sweet and kind and warm—which might explain why that kiss and her enthusiastic response had left him so discombobulated.

A few minutes later she finished at the sink and set the brushes to dry.

"I guess that's it," she said, still not looking at Flynn. "The brushes are all clean and ready for Hope when she has time to come down and finish. I'm just going to head up to the house to check on the cookie decorating. Thanks again for doing this, you guys."

She gave a vague, general sort of smile, then hurried out of the barn.

He and Rafe worked in silence for a few more moments, a heavy, thick tension in the air.

The other man was the first to speak.

"Do you know what happened to Celeste and her sisters when they were kids?"

Rafe's tone was casual, but the hard edge hadn't left his expression since he had walked into the work space earlier.

"In Colombia? Yeah. She told me. I can't imagine what they must have gone through."

Rafe's hard expression didn't lighten. "None of them talks about it very much. Frankly, I'm surprised she told you at all."

He didn't know why she had, but he was touched that she would confide that very significant part of her life to him.

He also didn't know why Rafe would bring it up now. It didn't seem the sort of topic to casually mention in general conversation. Something told him Rafe wasn't a man who did things without purpose.

"She was the youngest," the man went on. "Barely older than Louisa, only about twelve. Just a little kid, really."

His chest ached, trying to imagine that sweet vulnerability forced into such a traumatic situation. It was the same ache he had whenever he thought about Olivia watching her mother's murder.

"They went through hell while they were prisoners," Rafe went on. "The leader of the rebels was a psycho idiot bastard. He didn't give them enough to eat that entire month they were there, they were squished into squalid quarters, they were provided no medical care or decent protections from the elements, they underwent psychological torture. It's a wonder they made it through."

His hand tightened on the board he held, and he

wanted to swing it at something, hard. He didn't need to hear about this. It only seemed to heighten these strange, tender feelings in his chest.

"It affected all of them in various ways," Rafe went on. "But I think it was hardest on Celeste. She was so young and so very softhearted, from what Hope tells me. She's always been a dreamer, her head filled with stories and music. The conditions they were forced into must have been particularly harsh on an innocent young girl who couldn't really comprehend what was happening to her family."

The ache in his chest expanded. He hated that she had gone through it and wished, more than anything, that he could make it right for her.

"Why are you telling me this?"

Rafe gave him a steady look, as if weighing how to respond. He could see in his eyes that her brother-in-law knew exactly what they had been doing just before he walked in. Flynn fought the urge to tell the man to back off, that it was none of Rafe's damn business.

"I was there," Rafe finally said. "Did she tell you that?"

Flynn stared. "Where?"

"In Colombia. I was part of the SEAL team that rescued the Nichols family. It was my very first mission. A guy doesn't forget something like that."

Rafe was big and tough enough that somehow Flynn wasn't surprised he'd been a SEAL. He supposed the only remarkable thing about the situation was that the man seemed content now to live in a small town in Idaho, running a holiday attraction.

"So you saw their father get shot."

Rafe's jaw tightened. "Yeah. I saw it. And I saw Celeste weep and weep during the entire helicopter flight when she realized what had happened. I thought she would jump right out after her father."

Flynn swallowed at the image. After the past three months he hadn't thought he had much of his heart left to break, but he was most definitely wrong.

"I also shot two revolutionaries who were trying to keep us from leaving with them," Rafe went on. "You might, in fact, say I've had CeCe's back since she was eleven years old."

Yeah. The man definitely knew he had walked in on them kissing.

"She's very important to me," the other man said. "The whole Nichols family is mine now."

He met Flynn's gaze and held it as if he wanted to be perfectly clear. "And make no mistake. I protect what's mine."

He could choose to be offended, he supposed. He hadn't been called out for kissing a woman in...*ever*. Somehow he couldn't drum up anything but respect for Rafe. He was actually touched in an odd way, grateful that she had someone looking out for her.

"Warning duly noted." He made his own voice firm. "But anything between Celeste and me is just that. Between the two of us."

Rafe seemed to accept that. "I just don't want to see her hurt. Despite everything she's been through, CeCe somehow has still managed to retain a sweetness and a generosity you won't find in many people on this planet. If you mess with that, I won't be the only member of this family who won't be happy about it. Trust me. You do *not* want to tangle with the Nichols women."

This, more than anything else the man had said, resonated with truth. She had become a friend, someone he liked and respected. He didn't want to hurt her, either, but he couldn't see any other outcome. He had a business, a life in LA. Beyond that he wasn't in any position right now to start a new relationship with anyone, not when Olivia was still so needy.

He had made a mistake, kissing her. A mistake that couldn't happen again.

He gave the other man a steady look. "I got it. Thanks. Now can we just finish this job so I can grab my daughter and go home?"

After a moment, Rafe nodded and turned back to work, much to Flynn's relief.

The walk from the lodge to the main house helped a great deal to cool her flaming cheeks, but it didn't do much for the tumult inside her.

Oh, that kiss. How was she supposed to act around him now when she was afraid that every second she was near him she would be reliving those wild, hot moments in his arms? His hands on her skin, his mouth on hers, all those muscles pressing her against the cabinet.

She shivered in remembered reaction. How was she supposed to pretend her world just hadn't been rocked?

It had happened. She couldn't scrub those moments from her memory bank—indeed, she had a feeling they would haunt her for a long time—but surely she was mature enough to be able to interact with him in a polite, casual way. What other choice did she have?

When she reached the house, she drew in a deep breath, hoping all trace of those heated moments was gone from her features in case either of her eagle-eyed sisters was inside, then she pushed open the door.

The scents of cinnamon and pine and sugar cookies greeted her and the warmth of the house wrapped around her like one of Aunt Mary's hand-knitted scarves. As she stood in the entry, she had a sudden, familiar moment of deep gratitude for her aunt and uncle who had taken in three lost and grieving girls and given them safe shelter from the hard realities of life.

This was home. Her center.

Some of the storm inside her seemed to calm a bit. This was how she made it through, by focusing on what was important to her. Her family, her stories, the ranch. That was what mattered, not these fragile feelings growing inside her for Flynn and Olivia.

Before she could even hang up her coat, she heard the click of little paws on the floor. A moment later Linus burst into the room and greeted her merrily. She had nearly forgotten she'd brought him up to the house during the rehearsal to hang out with Mary, since Lucy had been in one of her snooty moods where she just wanted to be left alone.

"Hi, there. There's my darling boy." She scooped him up in her arms, and he licked her face and wriggled in her arms as if they had been away from each other for years instead of only a few hours.

"Have you been good?" she asked. He licked her cheek in answer, then wiggled to be let down again. She followed him and the sound of laughter to the kitchen, where she found her niece and nephews decorating cookies with Aunt Mary and Olivia.

"Look at all our cookies!" Barrett said. "The old people are going to *love* them."

He was such an adorable child, with a huge reservoir of compassion and love inside him for others.

This was a prime example—though she decided at some point she probably would have to gently inform him that the senior citizens coming to the show next week might not appreciate being called "old people."

"What a great job."

"Look at this one, Aunt CeCe. See how I made the stars sparkle with the yellow sugar things?" Joey, joined at the hip with Barrett, thrust his cookies at her.

"Fabulous."

"And look at my Christmas trees," Barrett said.

"I see. Good work, kid. And, Lou, I love how you swirled the icing on the candy canes. Very creative."

She turned to Olivia. "What about you? Have you decorated any?"

"A few." She pointed to a tray where a dozen angel cookies lay wing to wing. They all had hair of yellow frosting, just like the blonde and lovely Elise Chandler. Celeste had a feeling that wasn't a coincidence.

"I love them. They're beautiful, every one."

"Decorating cookies is *hard*," Joey declared. "You have to be careful you don't break them while you're putting on the frosting."

"But then you get to eat them when they break," Barrett pointed out.

"They've all been very good not to eat too many broken cookies," Aunt Mary said from the stove, where she was stirring something that smelled like her delicious ham-and-potato soup.

"Can you help us?" Louisa asked.

She had a million things to do before the show—not to mention a pile of unwrapped gifts in the corner of her office at home—but this suddenly seemed to take precedence over everything else.

"Of course," she answered her niece with a smile. "I can't imagine anything I would enjoy more."

Mary replaced the lid on the stockpot on the stove and turned down the burner. "Since you're here to supervise now, I think I'll go lie down and put my feet up. If you don't mind anyway. These swollen ankles are killing me today."

"Go ahead, my dear. You've done more than enough."

"I've got soup on the stove. The children had some earlier, but there's more than enough for anyone who pops in or out."

Celeste left the children busy at the table and headed over to hug her aunt before she reached in the cupboard for a bowl. "I know Hope and Rafe are back. I bumped into Rafe." She felt herself blush when she said it and hoped Aunt Mary wouldn't notice. "What about Faith? Is she around?"

"No. She ran into Idaho Falls for some last-minute g-i-f-t-s," Aunt Mary spelled, as if the children were tiny instead of excellent readers. Fortunately none of the children seemed to be paying attention to them.

"Poor girl," her aunt went on. "She's been too busy around the ranch to give Christmas much thought, and now here it is just a few days away."

The reminder instantly made Celeste feel small. She was fretting about a kiss while her sister had lost a husband and was raising two children by herself—albeit with plenty of help from Aunt Mary, Rafe, Hope and Celeste.

She was so grateful for her loving, supportive family—though she experienced a pang of regret for Flynn, who had no one.

She sat down at the table with her soup and listened to the children's chatter while she ate each delicious spoonful. When she finished, she set her bowl aside and turned to the serious business of cookie decorating.

"All right. Help me out, kids. What kind of cookie should I decorate first?"

"The angels are really hard," Olivia said.

Well, she'd already faced down a bunch of holiday-excited children and been kissed until she couldn't think straight. What was one more challenge today? "Bring on an angel, then."

Aunt Mary always had Christmas music playing in the house and the children seemed to enjoy singing along. Olivia didn't join them, she noticed. The girl seemed a little withdrawn, and Celeste worried maybe the day had been too much for her.

After she had decorated her third cookie, the song "Angels We Have Heard on High" came over the stereo.

"Ooh, I love this one," Louisa said. Her niece started singing along to the Glorias with a gusto that made Celeste smile.

"My mom is an angel now," Olivia said in a matter-of-fact sort of tone that made emotions clog Celeste's throat.

"I know, sweetheart," she said softly. "I'm so sorry."

"Our dad is an angel, too," Barrett informed her.

"Mom says he's probably riding the prettiest horses in heaven right now," Louisa said.

"My mom is in jail," Joey offered. That made her just as sad for him.

"Aren't you lucky to have Uncle Rafe and Aunt Hope, though?"

"Yep," he answered.

Barrett nodded. "And we still have our mom. And you have your dad," he reminded Olivia.

"Your mom *and* your dad are angels, aren't they?"

Louisa said to Celeste. "I asked my mom once why Barrett and me don't have a grandma and a grandpa, and she told me."

The pain of losing them still hurt, but more like an old ache than the constant, raw pain she remembered.

"They both died," she agreed. "It's been a long time, but I still feel them near me."

At some moments she felt them closer than others. She was quite certain she had heard her father's voice loud and clear one wintry, stormy night when she was driving home from college for the holidays. As clear as if he had been sitting beside her, she'd heard him tell her to slow down. She had complied instantly and a moment later rounded a corner to find a car had spun out from the opposite lane into hers. She was able to stop in time to keep from hitting it, but if she hadn't reduced her speed earlier, the head-on collision probably would have killed her and the other driver.

"Do you ever *see* your mom and dad angels?" Olivia asked, studying Celeste intently.

Oh, the poor, poor dear. She shook her head. "I don't see them as they were, but whenever I see the angel decorations at Christmastime, it helps me think about them and remember they're always alive in my heart."

"I really need to ask my mom something," Olivia said, her little features distressed. "Only I don't know how."

Celeste reached for the girl's hand and squeezed it. Oh, how she recalled all those unspoken words she had wanted to tell her parents, especially her father, who had died so abruptly. With her mother, she'd had a little more time, though that didn't ease the difficulty of losing her.

She chose her answer carefully, trying to find the right words of comfort.

"When you see an angel decoration you really like, perhaps you could whisper to the angel what you need to say to your mom. I believe she'll hear you," she said softly, hoping she was saying the right things to ease the girl's grief and not just offering a useless panacea.

Olivia considered that for a long moment, her brow furrowed. Finally she nodded solemnly. "That's a good idea. I think I'll do that."

She smiled and gave the girl a little hug, hoping she had averted that particular crisis. "Excellent. Now, why don't we see how many more cookies we can decorate before your father comes in?"

"Okay."

They went to work, singing along to the Christmas music for another half hour before the doorbell rang.

"I'll get it!" Joey announced eagerly. He raced for the door and a moment later returned with Flynn.

She had known it would be him at the door, but somehow she still wasn't prepared for the sheer masculine force of him. Suddenly she couldn't seem to catch her breath and felt as if the vast kitchen had shrunk to the size of one of Louisa's dollhouse rooms.

The memory of that kiss shivered between them, and she could feel heat soak her cheeks and nerves flutter in her stomach.

She shoved aside the reaction and forced a smile instead. "That was faster than I expected. Are you finished?" she asked.

He shrugged. "Your brother-in-law is a handy dude. With both of us working together, it didn't take us long."

"Wonderful. I can't tell you how much I appreciate it, especially with everything else you have going on. Thank you."

He met her gaze finally, and she thought she saw an instant of heat and hunger before he blinked it away. "You're very welcome."

His gaze took in the table scattered with frosting bowls, sugar sprinkles and candy nonpareils. "This looks fun," he said, though his tone implied exactly the opposite.

"Oh, it is, Daddy," Olivia declared. "Look at all the cookies I decorated! About a hundred angels!"

More like fifteen or sixteen, but Celeste supposed it had felt like much more than that to a seven-year-old girl.

She handed over one of the paper plates they had been using to set the decorated cookies on when they were finished. "Here, fill this with several cookies so you and your dad can take some home to enjoy."

"They're for the old people, though, aren't they?"

"I think it would be just fine for you to take five or six. We'll have plenty. Don't worry," she answered, declining again to give a lecture on politically correct terminology.

"Are you sure?"

"Yes. Go ahead. Pick some of your favorites."

Olivia pondered her options and finally selected five cookies—all blonde angels, Celeste noted—and laid them on the paper plate while Celeste found some aluminum foil to cover them.

"Here you go," she said, holding them out to Flynn.

"Thanks," he murmured and took the plate from her. Their hands brushed and she gave an involuntary shiver that she seriously hoped he hadn't noticed.

His gaze met hers for just an instant, then slid away again, but not before she saw a glittery, hungry look there that made her feel breathless all over again.

"Find your coat," he told his daughter.

"Can we stay a little bit longer?" Olivia begged. "Louisa and Barrett and Joey said they're going to have sleigh rides later. I've never been on a sleigh ride."

"We have a lot to do today, bug. We've already hung around here longer than we probably should have."

If he and his daughter had left earlier, the kiss never would have happened. Judging by the edgy tension that seethed between them now—and despite the flash of hunger she thought she had glimpsed—Celeste had a feeling that was what he would have preferred.

"Please, Daddy. I would *love* it."

As he gazed at his daughter a helpless look came into his eyes. She remembered him saying he hated refusing Olivia anything after what she had been through.

"How long do these sleigh rides take?" he asked Celeste.

"Less than an hour, probably."

"They're super fun at night," her niece suggested helpfully. "You could go home and do your work and then come back later. Then you can see all the lights and stuff. There's even caroling."

"Ooh. Caroling!" Olivia looked delighted at the idea, while her father looked vaguely horrified.

"I must agree. It is really fun," Celeste said.

He sighed. "Would that work for you, Liv? We can go home and try to finish another room at the house, and then come back later."

"Will you all be there?" she asked her new friends.

"Sure! We love to take the sleigh rides."

Olivia looked enchanted by the idea.

"Our last sleigh ride for regular visitors of The Christmas Ranch is back at the St. Nicholas Lodge about 8:00 p.m.

Why don't you meet us at the lodge a little before that, and we can take one that's not as crowded?"

"Oh, yay! I can't wait!" Olivia exclaimed. She spontaneously hugged Celeste, and she looked so adorably sweet with her eyes bright and pink frosting on her cheek that Celeste couldn't help it, she kissed the top of the girl's head.

When she lifted her head, she found Flynn gazing at her with a strange look on his features that he quickly wiped away.

"I guess we'll see you all later tonight, then," he said.

He didn't sound nearly as thrilled as his daughter about the idea.

Chapter Eleven

All afternoon Celeste did her best not to dwell on that stunning kiss.

Knowing she would see him again that evening didn't help. The whole busy December day seemed filled with sparkly anticipation, even though she tried over and over again to tell herself she was being ridiculous.

It didn't help matters that her sisters both attempted to back out of the sleigh ride and send her alone with the children. She couldn't blame them, since it had been completely her idea, but she still wanted them there. Though she knew the children would provide enough of a buffer, she didn't want to be alone with Flynn.

Finally she had threatened Hope that if she didn't go on the sleigh ride with them, Hope would have to direct the show Tuesday night by herself.

As she expected, Rafe had obviously told Hope what

he had almost walked in on earlier in the barn. Her sisters hadn't come out and said anything specific about it, but after the third or fourth speculative look from Hope— and the same from Faith—she knew the word was out in the Nichols family.

If not for her beloved niece and nephews, she sincerely would have given some thought to wishing she had been an only child.

"You owe me this after dragging me into the whole Christmas show thing," Celeste said fiercely to Hope at dinner, when her sister once more tried to wriggle out of the sleigh ride.

Hope didn't necessarily look convinced, but she obviously could see that Celeste meant what she said. "Oh, all right," she muttered. "If I'm going out in the cold that means you have to come, too, Fae."

Faith groaned. "After an afternoon of tackling the stores on the busiest shopping day of the year, I just want to put my feet up and watch something brainless on TV."

Barrett added his voice. "You *have* to come, Mom. It won't be as fun without you. You've got the *best* caroling voice."

"Yeah, and you're the only one who knows all the words," Louisa added.

Faith gave her children an exasperated look but finally capitulated. "Fine. I guess somebody has to help you all carry a tune."

After dinner they all bundled up in their warmest clothing and traipsed down to the St. Nicholas Lodge. Even Rafe came along, which she supposed she was grateful for, though he kept shooting her curious little looks all evening.

They arrived at the lodge just as Flynn and Olivia

walked in from the parking lot. Olivia wore her pink-and-purple coat with a white beanie and scarf. She looked adorable, especially when she lit up at the sight of them.

"Hi, everybody! Hi!" she said. "We're here. Dad didn't want to come, but I told him we promised, so here we are."

Celeste had to laugh at that, especially when Flynn's color rose. "It's good to see you both," she said.

It wasn't a lie. The December night suddenly seemed magical and bright, filled with stars and snow and the wonder of the season.

Olivia skipped over to her, hardly even limping in her excitement for the evening. "Guess what, Celeste?"

"What, sweetheart?"

"Today when we were cleaning we found boxes and boxes and *boxes* of yarn and scrapbook paper and craft supplies. Would you like to have them for your story times at the library? Dad said he thought you might."

"Seriously?" She stared, overwhelmed and touched that he would think of it.

"You don't have to take them," he said quickly. "I just didn't want to send everything to Goodwill if you could find a use for it."

"Are you kidding?" she exclaimed. "Absolutely! I can definitely use craft supplies. Thank you so much!"

"Good, because they're all in the back of the SUV. I took a chance that you would want them and figured if you didn't, I could drop them in the box at the thrift store in town after we were done here."

"Smart." She considered their options. "My car is still here in the parking lot from this morning. I can just pull next to you, and we can transfer them from your SUV to mine."

"Do you want to do it now or after the sleigh ride?"

"Go ahead and do it now while you're thinking about it," Hope suggested. Celeste narrowed her gaze at her sister, wondering if this was some sneaky way to get the two of them alone together, but Hope merely gave her a bland look in response.

"Sure," she said finally. "That way we won't forget later."

They walked out into the cold air, and she tried not to think about the last time they had been together—the strength of his muscles beneath her hands, the delicious taste of him, all those shivery feelings he evoked.

"I'm parked over there," he said, pointing to his vehicle.

"I parked at the back of the lot this morning to leave room for paying guests. Just give me a minute to move my car next to yours."

"I could just carry the boxes over to where you are."

"It will only take me a minute to move." She took off before he could argue further and hurried to her very cold vehicle, which had a thin layer of soft snow that needed to be brushed away before she could see out the windshield. Once that was done, she started it and drove the few rows to an open spot next to his vehicle, then popped open the hatch of her small SUV.

By the time she opened her door and walked around to the back, he was already transferring boxes and she could see at least half dozen more in the back of his vehicle.

She stared at the unexpected bounty. "This is amazing! Are you sure Olivia wouldn't like to keep some of this stuff?"

He shook his head. "She went through and picked out a few pairs of decorative scissors and some paper she really liked, but the rest of it was destined for either Good-will or the landfill."

"Thank you. It was really kind of you to think of the library."

"Consider it a legacy from Charlotte to the library."

"I'll do that. Thank you."

He carried the last of the boxes and shoved it into her cargo area, then closed the hatch.

"There you go."

"Thanks again."

She expected him to head directly back to the lodge. Instead, he leaned against her vehicle and gave her a solemn look. The parking lot was mostly empty except for a family a few rows away loading into a minivan, probably after seeing Santa Claus inside.

"Do I owe you an apology?" he asked.

She fidgeted, shoving her mittened hands into her pockets. "An apology for what?"

He sighed. "We both know I shouldn't have kissed you, Celeste. It was a mistake. I didn't want to leave you with the...wrong impression."

Oh, this was humiliating. Was she so pathetic that he thought because she had told him she'd once had a crush on him, she now thought they were *dating* or something, because of one stupid kiss?

Okay, one *amazing*, heart-pounding, knee-tingling kiss. But that was beside the point.

"You don't owe me anything," she said.

He gazed up at the stars while the jingle of the sleigh returning to the lodge and the sound of shrieking children over on the sledding hill rang out in the distance.

"Here's the thing. Right now, my whole attention has

to be focused on helping my daughter. I'm not…looking for anything else. I can't."

She leaned against the cold vehicle next to him and tried to pretend she was sophisticated and experienced, that this sort of moment happened to her all the time—a casual conversation with a man who had kissed her deeply just a few hours ago and was now explaining why he couldn't do it again.

"It was a kiss, Flynn. I get it. I've barely given it a thought since it happened."

He wasn't stupid. She didn't doubt he could tell that was a blatant lie, but he said nothing. He simply gave her a careful look, which she returned with what she hoped was a bland one of her own.

"Good. That's good," he said. "I just wanted to clear the air between us. The last thing I want to do is hurt you or, I don't know, give you the wrong idea. You've been nothing but kind to Olivia and to me."

"Do you really think I'm so fragile that I could be hurt by a single kiss?"

The question seemed to hang between them, bald and unadorned, like a bare Christmas tree after the holidays.

He had a fierce wish that he'd never started this conversation, but the implications of that kiss had bothered him all afternoon as he'd carried box after box out of Charlotte's house.

He meant what he said. She had been very sweet to him and Olivia. His daughter was finally beginning to heal from the trauma she had endured, and he knew a big part of the progress she'd made the past week was because of all the many kindnesses Celeste and her family had shown them.

It seemed a poor repayment for him to take advantage of that because he couldn't control his base impulses around her.

He also couldn't seem to shake the guilt that had dogged him since that conversation with Rafe. The other man hadn't come out and blatantly told him to leave her alone, but Flynn hadn't missed the subtle undercurrents.

"Your brother-in-law and I had quite a talk this afternoon while we were finishing the screens for you."

"Is that right?"

Her cheeks looked pink in the moonlight, but he supposed that could have been from the cold night air.

"He's very protective of you and wanted to be clear I knew you had people watching out for you."

She made a low noise in the back of her throat. "My family sometimes drives me absolutely crazy."

Despite the awkwardness of the conversation, he had to smile. "They're wonderful, all of them. It's obvious they love you very much."

"A little too much, sometimes," she muttered. "They apparently don't think I can be trusted to take care of myself. Sometimes it really sucks to be the youngest sibling."

He couldn't imagine having any siblings. While he was lucky to have very tight friends, he knew it wasn't the same.

"I think it's nice," he answered. "Having your sisters close must have been a great comfort after you lost your parents."

Her lovely features softened in the moonlight. "It was," she murmured. "They may drive me crazy, but I would be lost without them. Don't tell them I said that, though."

He smiled a little. "I wish I had that same kind of support network for Olivia, but I'm all she has right now. I can't forget that."

"I understand. You're doing a great job with her. Don't worry. Children are resilient. She's working her way over to the other side in her own time."

His sigh puffed out condensation between them. "Thanks."

"And you can put your mind at ease," she said briskly. "You're not going to break my heart. Trust me, I don't have some crazy idea that you're going to propose to me simply because we shared one little kiss."

"It wasn't a little kiss. That's the problem," he muttered.

As soon as he said the words, he knew he shouldn't have, but it was the truth. That kiss had been earthshaking. Cataclysmic. He would venture to call it epic, which was the entire problem here. He knew he wouldn't forget those moments for a long, long time.

He wasn't sure how he expected her to respond but, as usual, she managed to surprise him. She flashed him a sideways look.

"What can I say? I'm a good kisser."

The unexpectedness of her response surprised a laugh out of him that echoed through the night. She seemed like such a sweet, quiet woman, but then she had these moments of sly humor that he couldn't seem to get enough of.

It made him wonder if she had this whole secret internal side of herself—contained and bundled away for protection—that she rarely showed the rest of the world.

She intrigued him on so many levels, probably because she was a study in contradictions. She could be tart and sweet at the same time, firm yet gentle, deeply vulnerable yet tough as nails.

Most of all, she seemed *real*. For a guy who had grown up surrounded by the artificial illusion of Hollywood, that was intensely appealing.

"It looks as if the other sleigh ride is done," she finally said. "The kids are probably anxious to get going."

"Right. Guess I'd better get my carol on."

She laughed, as he had hoped. At least the tension between them since the afternoon had been somewhat diffused.

As they walked, he was aware of a jumble of feelings in his chest. Regret, longing and a strange, aching tenderness.

For just a moment, he had a crazy wish that things could be different, that he had the right to wrap his hand around hers and walk up to the sleigh ride with her, then sit beneath a blanket cuddled up with her while they rode in a horse-drawn sleigh and enjoyed the moonlit wonder of the night together.

He could handle the regret and the longing. He was a big boy and had known plenty of disappointments in his life.

But he didn't have any idea what to do with the tenderness.

Celeste decided a sleigh ride through the mountains on a December evening was a good metaphor for being in love.

She was bumped and jostled, her face cold but the rest of her warm from the blankets. It was exhilarating and exhausting, noisy and fun and a little bit terrifying when they went along a narrow pass above the ranch that was only two feet wider on each side than the sleigh.

She'd been on the sleigh ride dozens of times before. This was the first time she'd taken one while also being in love, with these tangled, chaotic feelings growing inside her.

She was quickly reaching the point where she couldn't deny that she was falling hard for Flynn. What else could explain this jumbled, chaotic mess of emotions inside her?

"Oh. Look at all those stars," a voice breathed beside her, and she looked down to where Olivia had her face lifted to the sky.

She wasn't only falling for Flynn. This courageous, wounded girl had sneaked her way into Celeste's heart.

She would be devastated when they left.

When they'd climbed into the sleigh, Olivia had asked if she could sit beside Celeste. The two of them were sharing a warm blanket. Every once in a while the girl rested her cheek against her shoulder, and Celeste felt as if her heart would burst with tenderness.

"I never knew there were so many stars," Olivia said, her voice awestruck.

"It's magical, isn't it?" she answered. "Do you know what I find amazing? That all those stars are there every single night, wherever you are in the world. They're just hidden by all the other lights around that distract us away from them."

The whole evening truly *was* magical—the whispering jingle of the bells on the draft horses' harnesses, the creak of the old sleigh, the sweet scent of the snow-covered pines they rode through.

Except for Mary—who had stayed behind in the warm house—Celeste was surrounded by everyone she loved.

"I wish we could just go and go and never stop," Olivia said.

Unfortunately, the magic of sleigh rides never lasted forever. She had a feeling that, at least in her case, the magic of being in love wouldn't last, either. The *in love* part would, but eventually the heartache would steal away any joy.

"We'll have to stop at some point," the ever-practical Faith said. "The horses are tired. They've been working all night and are probably ready to have a rest."

"Besides that," Joey added, "what would we eat if we were stuck on a sleigh our whole lives?"

"Good point, kid," Rafe said. "We can't live on hot chocolate forever."

Olivia giggled at them and seemed to concede their point.

"I thought we were supposed to be caroling. We haven't sung *anything*," Louisa complained.

"You start us off," her mother suggested.

Celeste was aware that while both her sisters seemed to be dividing careful looks between her and Flynn, they did it at subtle moments. If she were very lucky, he wouldn't notice.

Louisa started, predictably enough, with "Jingle Bells." The children joined in with enthusiasm and soon even the adults joined them. Flynn, on the other side of Olivia, had a strong baritone. Under other circumstances, she might have been entranced by it, but Celeste's attention was fixed on his daughter as she sang.

Why hadn't she noticed during their rehearsals and the songs they had prepared that Olivia had such a stunning voice, pure and clear, like a mountain stream? It was perfectly on pitch, too, astonishing in a child.

She wasn't the only one who noticed it, she saw. Hope and Faith both seemed startled and even Rafe gave her a second look.

Flynn didn't seem to notice anything, and she thought of those stars again, vivid and bright but obscured by everything else in the way.

"What next?" Joey asked. "Can we sing the one about Jolly Old St. Nick?"

"Sure," Faith said. Of the three sisters, she had the most musical ability, so she led the children as the sleigh bells jingled through the night. With each song, Olivia's natural musical talent became increasingly apparent to everyone on the sleigh, but both she and Flynn seemed oblivious.

"What's that place with all the lights?" Olivia asked after they finished "Silent Night."

"That's the Christmas village," Barrett answered her. "It's awesome. Can we stop and walk through it?"

"You've seen it, like, a million times," his sister chided.

"Yeah, but Olivia hasn't. It's way more fun to see it with somebody else who has never been there. It's like seeing it for the first time all over again."

"You are so right, kiddo," Hope said, beaming at the boy. "Bob, do you mind dropping us off here so we can take a little detour through the village?"

"Not at all. Not at all."

The driver pulled the team to a stop, and everybody clambered out of the sleigh and headed toward the collection of eight small structures a short distance from the main lodge.

This was one of her favorite parts of the entire Christmas Ranch. With the lights strung overhead, it really did feel magical.

Each structure contained a Christmas scene peopled with animatronic figures—elves hammering toys, Mrs. Claus baking cookies, children decorating a Christmas tree, a family opening presents.

"This is quite a place," Flynn murmured beside her.

"The Christmas village is really what started the whole Christmas Ranch. You probably don't know this, but my family's name of origin was Nicholas. As in St. Nicholas."

"The big man himself."

"Right. Because of that, my aunt and uncle have always been a little crazy about Christmas. Before we came to live with them, my uncle Claude built the little chapel Nativity over there with the cow who nods his head at the baby Jesus and the two little church mice running back and forth. It became a hobby with him, and after that he came up with a new one every year."

With a pang, she dearly missed her uncle, a big, gruff man of such kindness and love. He had taught her and her sisters that the best way to heal a broken heart was to forget your troubles and go to work helping other people.

"He decided he wanted to share the village with the whole community, so he opened the ranch up for people to come and visit. The reindeer herd came after, and then he built the whole St. Nicholas Lodge for Santa Claus, and the gift shop and everything."

"This is really great. I have no idea how he did it. It's a fascinating exercise in engineering and physics."

She frowned up at the star above the chapel, just a dark outline against the mountains. "Usually the star up there lights up. I'm not sure what's wrong with it. I'll have to mention it to Rafe. He has learned the ins and outs of all the structures in the village. I don't know how everything works. I just love the magic of it."

Olivia appeared to agree. The girl seemed enthralled with the entire village, particularly the little white chapel with its Nativity scene—the calm Madonna cradling her infant son, and Joseph watching over them both with such care while a beautiful angel with sparkly white wings watched overhead.

"You guys are welcome to hang out, but we're going to head back to the house," Faith said after about fifteen minutes. "It's cold and I know my two are about ready for bed."

"We need to go, too," Hope said, pointing to a sleepy-looking Joey.

"Thank you all for taking us on one more ride," Flynn said. "I appreciate it very much. Olivia loved it."

"You're very welcome," Hope said. "It was our pleasure."

The rest of her family headed back up to the ranch house while Celeste and Flynn walked with Olivia to the lodge's parking lot.

"I'm glad you both came," Celeste said when they reached their vehicles.

"This is definitely a memory we'll have forever, isn't it, Liv?" Flynn said as he opened the backseat door for his daughter. "When we're back in California enjoying Christmas by the ocean, we'll always remember the year we went caroling through the mountains on a two-horse open sleigh."

She had to smile, even though his words seemed to cut through her like an icy wind whipping down the mountain.

"We'll see you Tuesday for the performance."

He nodded, though he didn't look thrilled.

"We'll be there. Thanks again."

She nodded and climbed into her own vehicle, trying not to notice how empty and cold it felt after the magic of being with them on the sleigh ride.

Chapter Twelve

"Are you sure we're not too early?" Flynn asked his daughter as they pulled up in front of the St. Nicholas Lodge on the night of the show. "It doesn't start for quite a while."

She huffed out her frustrated-at-Dad sigh. "I'm sure. She told me five thirty. This is when I'm supposed to be here, Celeste said, so they can help me get ready with my hair and makeup and stuff. I get to wear makeup onstage so my face isn't blurry."

Yeah, he was terrible with hair and didn't have the first idea what to do about makeup. Here was a whole new stress about having a daughter. Soon enough she was going to want to know about that stuff. Good thing he had friends in LA with wives who could help a poor single dad out in that department.

She opened the passenger door the moment he pulled

into a parking space. "Okay. Thanks, Dad. I'll see you at the show."

When he turned off the engine and opened his own door, she gave him a look of surprise. "You don't have to come in yet."

He shrugged. "I'm here. I might as well see if they need help with something—setting up chairs or whatever."

"Okay," she said, then raced for the door without waiting to see if he followed. Clearly, he was far more nervous about this whole performance thing than she was.

She had made amazing progress in a short time. In a matter of days she already seemed much more at ease with herself and the world around her than she had been when he brought her to Pine Gulch. She used her arm almost without thinking about it now, and she hardly limped anymore.

He wasn't foolish to think all the pain and grief were behind them. She would be dealing with the trauma for a long time to come, but he was beginning to hope that they had turned a corner.

Children are resilient. She's working her way over to the other side in her own time.

He gave no small amount of credit to the Nichols family, for their warmth and acceptance of her. She had made friends with the children and she also completely adored Celeste.

Would he be able to keep that forward momentum when they returned to California? He had no idea, but he would sure as hell try—even if that meant figuring out the whole hair-and-makeup thing on his own sometime down the line.

He pushed open the front doors after her and walked

into the lodge, only to discover the place had been transformed into an upscale-looking dining room.

What had been an open space was now filled with
round eight-top tables wearing silky red tablecloths and
evergreen and candle centerpieces. The huge Christmas
tree in the corner blazed with color and light, joined by
merry fires flickering in the river-rock fireplaces at both
ends of the vast room. Glittery white lights stretched
across the room and gleamed a welcome.

The air smelled delicious—ham and yeasty rolls and,
if he wasn't mistaken, apple pie.

Like iron shavings to a magnet, his gaze instantly
found Celeste. She was right in the middle of everything,
directing a crew of caterers while they laid out table settings.

His stomach muscles tightened. She looked beautiful,
with her hair up in a dark, elegant sweep and wearing a
simple tailored white blouse and green skirt. Again, the
alluring contradictions. She looked prim and sexy at the
same time.

"Hi, Celeste," Olivia chirped, heading straight to her
for a hug, which was readily accepted and returned.

He didn't understand the bond between the two of
them, but he couldn't deny the strength of it.

"Looks as if you've been busy," he said, gesturing to
the tables.

"Hope and Rafe did all this while I was working at
the library today. It looks great, doesn't it?"

"Wonderful," he agreed. "I was going to see if there
was anything I could do to help, but you seem to have
everything under control."

"I don't know if I'd go that far," she answered with a
rather frazzled-sounding laugh. "I don't know what I was

thinking to agree to this. If Hope ever tries to rope me into one of her harebrained ideas again, please remind me of this moment and my solemn vow that I will never be so gullible again."

He smiled even as he was aware of a sharp ache in his chest. He wouldn't be around to remind her of anything. Some other guy would be the one to do that—a realization that he suddenly hated.

"Thanks for bringing Olivia early. She wanted her hair fixed the same as Louisa's."

"She said it was going to be a big bun on her head," Olivia said. "That's what I want."

Celeste smiled at her. "Find your costume first, and then Louisa's mom is on hair and makeup duty in the office, and she'll help you out."

"Okay," she said eagerly, then trotted away.

Without the buffer of his daughter, he suddenly couldn't escape the memory of that earthshaking kiss a few days earlier. When she smiled like that, her eyes huge behind her glasses, he wanted to reach out, tug her against him and taste her one more time.

"How are you?" she asked.

He didn't know how to answer. That strange, irresistible tenderness seemed to twist and curl through him like an unruly vine. As he had no idea what to do with it, he said the first thing he could think of in a futile effort to put distance between them.

"Good. It's been a busy few days. We've made a lot of progress with Charlotte's house. We're now down to one room and a few cupboards here and there."

She didn't answer for about three beats, and he thought he saw her hand tighten. Would she miss them when they left? Olivia, no doubt. What about him?

"That's a huge job," she finally said. "I imagine you must be relieved to be nearing the finish line."

Relieved? No. Not really. It had been a strange, disquieting experience sorting through the pieces of his grandparents' lives, all the treasures and papers and worthless junk they had left behind. It made a man wonder what would remain of his own life once he was gone. Right now he didn't feel as though he had all that much to show for his years on the planet.

"I thought it would take me until at least New Year's, but we're ahead of schedule."

"That's great," she said. Was that cheerful note in her voice genuine or forced?

"At this point, I'm thinking we'll probably take off the day after Christmas. Maybe we'll drive to San Diego for a few days before we head back up the coast to LA."

"Oh. So soon? I... That will be nice for you, to be back in the warmth and sunshine after all this snow we've had."

Logically, he knew it *should* be what he wanted, to go home and begin cobbling together the rest of their lives, but he still couldn't manage to drum up much enthusiasm for it.

"If I don't get the chance to talk to you again, I wanted to be sure to give you my thanks for all you've done to help Olivia."

Surprise flickered in those lovely eyes. "I didn't do anything," she protested.

"You know that's not true," he said. "You have been nothing but kind to her from the first moment we met you at the library that day. You gave her an unforgettable birthday celebration and have helped her feel the Christmas spirit when I would have thought that impossible this year. She's beginning to return to her old self, and I give a great deal of the credit for that to you and your family."

Her smile was soft and sweet and lit up her face like a thousand twinkly lights. He was struck again by how truly lovely she was, one of those rare women who became more beautiful the more times a man saw her.

"She's a remarkable girl, Flynn. I feel honored to have had the chance to know her. I'll miss her. I'll miss both of you."

Before he could come up with a reply to that—before he could do something stupid like tell her how very much he would miss her, too—one of the catering crew came up to her to ask a question about the dessert trays. After an awkward little pause, she excused herself to help solve the problem.

I'll miss her. I'll miss both of you.

The words seemed to echo through the vast lodge. While his daughter's life had been changed for the better because of their stay here in Pine Gulch, he wasn't sure he could say the same thing for his own.

He would miss Celeste, too. Rather desperately, he realized suddenly. As he stood in her family's holiday lodge surrounded by the trappings of the season, he realized how very much she had impacted his world, too.

"Got a minute?"

He had been so lost in thought he hadn't notice Rafe come in. Though there was still a certain wariness between the two of them, Rafe seemed to have become much more accepting of him after their time together working in the barn the other day.

He liked and respected the other man. In fact, Flynn suspected that if he and Olivia *were* to stick around Pine Gulch, he and Rafe would have become friends.

"I have more than a minute," he answered. "I'm just the chauffeur right now, apparently, delivering Olivia to get her hair fixed."

"Perfect. While you've got your chauffeur hat on, I've got about twenty older ladies in need of rides. None of them likes to drive after dark, apparently, and especially not when it's snowing. Naturally, Hope promised them all she would find a way to get them here without thinking of the impossible logistics of the thing. Chase was supposed to help me shuttle them all, but he got tied up with something at his ranch and won't be free until right before the show starts. Everybody else is busy right now with the kids, so I'm in a pinch."

He was honored to be asked, even though he wasn't part of the community. "Sure. I'm happy to help, but I don't know where anybody lives. You'll have to tell me where to go."

"I've got a list right here with addresses and names. I figure if we split it up, we'll have time to get everybody here before the show, but it's going to be tight. You sure you don't mind?"

He didn't. It felt good to be part of something, to feel as though he was giving back a little for all that had been done for him and Olivia.

"Not at all. Let's do it."

"Where's my dad?" Olivia asked. "I thought he was going to be here to watch."

She looked absolutely beautiful in the little angel costume she wore for the show—and for the special part they had just practiced at the last minute.

The costume set off her delicate features and lovely blond hair to perfection.

Celeste's gaze drifted from her to the other children in their costumes. They all looked completely adorable. Somehow, by a Christmas miracle, they were really going to pull this off.

"Do you see my dad?" Olivia asked.

She frowned and looked around the beautiful screens Rafe and Flynn had built to serve as the wings to their small stage. She saw many familiar, beloved neighbors and friends, but no sign of a certain gorgeous man.

"I can't see him, but I'm sure he'll be here."

"Who are you looking for?" Hope asked, looking up from adjusting Joey's crooked crown.

"Flynn."

"I don't think he's back yet from picking up the last group of ladies."

Celeste stared at her sister. "What ladies?"

"Oh, didn't you know? Rafe asked him to help shuttle some of the ladies who wanted to come to the dinner and show, but didn't want to be stuck driving after dark."

She gaped at her sister. "Seriously? Flynn?"

"Yeah. He's already dropped off one carload earlier, and then I think Rafe sent him out again."

She pictured him driving through the snow to pick up a bunch of older ladies he didn't even know, and her throat seemed suddenly tight and achy. What a darling he was, to step up where he was needed.

How was she supposed to be able to resist a man like that?

She was in love with him.

She drew in a shaky breath as the reality of it crashed over her as if the entire plywood set had just tumbled onto her head. It was quite possible that she had been in love with him since that summer afternoon so many years ago when he had picked her up from her bike, dried her tears and cleaned up her scratches and scrapes.

Was that the reason she had never really become serious about any of the other men she dated in college? She'd always told herself she wasn't ready, that she didn't feel comfortable with any of them, that she was too socially awkward. That all might have been true, but perhaps the underlying reason was because she had already given her heart to the larger-than-life boy he had been.

In the past few weeks she truly had come to know him as more than just a kind teenager, her secret fantasy of what a hero should be. She had come to admire so many other things about him. His strength, his goodness, the love he poured out to his daughter.

How could she *not* love such a wonderful man? She loved him and she loved Olivia, too. Her heart was going to shatter into a million tiny pieces when they left.

"What if he doesn't make it back?" Olivia fretted now. "He'll miss my big surprise."

Celeste drew in a breath and forced herself to focus on the show. There would be time for heartbreak later.

"He'll make it back. Don't worry. He wouldn't miss seeing you."

Actually, Flynn missing Olivia's big surprise might not be such a bad thing. She wasn't quite sure he would like it, but it was too late for regrets now.

Olivia still seemed edgy as the music started. Her uneven gait was more pronounced than usual as she followed the other children onstage for their opening number.

Just as the last child filed on, she saw him leading three older women: Agnes Sheffield, her sister and their friend Dolores Martinez.

She watched around the wings as he took their coats, then helped them find empty seats. Agnes touched his arm in a rather coquettish way. As he gave the octogenarian an amused smile, Celeste fell a little in love with him all over again.

Darn man. Why did he have to be so wonderful?

At last, when everyone was settled and the children were standing on the risers, Destry Bowman, one of the older girls, took the microphone.

"We welcome you all to the first ever holiday extravaganza at The Christmas Ranch. Consider this our Christmas gift to each of you."

The children immediately launched into the show, which was mostly a collection of familiar songs with a few vignette skits performed by the older children. After only a few moments, she could tell it was going to be considered an unqualified success.

She saw people laughing in all the right parts, catching their breath in expectation, even growing teary eyed at times, just as she'd predicted to the children. Most of all, she hoped they had a little taste of the joy and magic of the season, which seemed so much more real when experienced through the eyes of a child.

This was different from writing a book. Here she could see the immediate impact of what she had created and helped produce.

Seeing that reaction in real time made her rethink her objections to the upcoming Sparkle movie. Maybe it wouldn't be such a bad thing. The story was about finding the joy and wonder of Christmas through helping others, as Uncle Claude and Aunt Mary had taught them. If Sparkle could help spread that message, she didn't see how she could stand in the way.

Finally, it was time for the last number, which they had changed slightly at the last minute.

"Are you ready, sweetheart?" she whispered to Olivia.

The girl nodded, the tinsel halo of her angel costume waving eagerly.

As all the children were onstage, she stepped out to the audience so she could watch. From this vantage point, she had a clear view of Flynn. His brow furrowed in confusion at first to see Olivia at the microphone, then when the piano player gave her a note for pitch and she started singing the first verse to "Silent Night" by herself a cappella, his features went tight and cold.

Her voice was pure and beautiful, as it had been the other night while they were caroling, and she sang the familiar song with clarity and sweetness. She saw a few people whispering and pointing and thought she saw Agnes Sheffield mouth the words *Elise Chandler* to Dolores.

When Olivia finished, the piano started and all the children sang the second verse with her, then Destry Bowman signaled the audience to join in on the third.

What they might have lacked in musical training or even natural ability, the children made up for in enthusiasm and bright smiles.

Beside her, Hope sniffled. "They're wonderful, CeCe. The whole show is so good."

She smiled, even though emotions clogged her own throat.

They finished to thunderous applause, which thrilled the children. She saw delight on each face, especially the proud parents.

A moment later, Hope took the stage to wrap up

things. "Let's give these amazing kids another round of applause," she said.

The audience readily complied, which made the children beam even more. The show had been a smashing success—which probably meant Hope would want to make it a tradition.

"I have to give props to one more person," she went on. To Celeste's shock, Hope looked straight at her. "My amazing sister, Celeste. Once again, she has taken one of my harebrained ideas and turned it into a beautiful reality. Celeste."

Her sister held out her hand for her to come onstage. She had never wanted to do some serious hair pulling more than she did at right that moment.

She thought about being obstinate and remaining right where she was, but that would only be even *more* awkward. With no choice in the matter, she walked onstage to combined applause from the performers and the audience.

Face blazing, she hurried back down the stairs and off stage as quickly as possible, in time to hear Hope's last words to the audience.

"Now, Jenna McRaven and her crew have come up with an amazing meal for you all, so sit back and enjoy. Parents, your kids are going to change out of their costumes and they'll be right out to join you for dinner. As a special treat for you, the wonderful Natalie Dalton and Lucy Boyer are going to entertain you during dinner with a duet for piano and violin."

The two cousins by marriage came out and started the low-key dinner music Hope had arranged while the caterers began serving the meal.

"You all did wonderfully," Celeste told the cast when they gathered offstage. "Thank you so much for your hard work. I'm so proud of you! Now hurry and change then come out and find your family so you can enjoy all this yummy food."

With much laughing and talking, the children rushed to the two dressing rooms they had set aside. She was picking up someone's discarded shepherd's crook when her sister Faith came around the screen.

"Great work, CeCe. It was truly wonderful." She gave one of her rare smiles, and in that moment, all the frenetic work seemed worth it.

"I'm glad it's over. Next year it's your turn."

"Great idea." Hope joined them and turned a speculative look in Faith's direction.

"Ha. That will be the day," Faith said. "Unlike Celeste, I know how to say no to you. I've been doing it longer."

Celeste laughed and hugged her sisters, loving them both dearly, then she hurried back into the hallway to help return costumes to hangers and hurry the children along.

Just before she reached the dressing room, Flynn caught up with her, his face tight with an emotion she couldn't quite identify.

Still caught up in the exhilaration of a job well done, she impulsively hugged him. "Oh, Flynn. Wasn't Olivia wonderful? She didn't have an ounce of stage fright. She's amazing."

He didn't hug her back and it took a moment for her to realize that emotion on his face wasn't enthusiasm. He was furious.

"Why didn't you tell me she was going to sing a solo?"

She didn't know how to answer. The truth was, she *had* worried about his reaction but had ignored the little niggling unease. For his own reasons, Flynn objected to his daughter performing at all, let alone by herself.

But the girl's voice was so lovely, Celeste had wanted her to share it.

Her heart sank, and she realized she had no good defense. "I should have told you," she admitted. "It was a last-minute thing. After we went caroling and I heard what a lovely voice she had, I decided to change the program slightly. I didn't have a lot of time to fill you in on the details since we decided to make the change just tonight, but I should have tried harder."

"You couldn't leave well enough alone. I told you I didn't want her doing the show in the first place, but my feelings didn't seem to matter. You pushed and pushed until I agreed, and then you threw her onto center stage, even though I made my feelings on it clear."

"She loved it!" she protested. "She wasn't nervous at all. A week ago, she was freaking out in a restaurant over a bin of dropped dishes, and today she was standing in front of a hundred people singing her heart out without flinching. I think that's amazing progress!"

"Her progress or lack of progress is none of your business. You understand? She's my daughter. I get to make those choices for her, not some small-town librarian who barely knows either of us."

She inhaled sharply as his words sliced and gouged at her like carving knives.

Her face suddenly felt numb, as frozen as her brain. That was all she was to him. A small-town librarian who didn't even know him or his daughter. It was as if all the closeness they had shared these past few days, the tender moments, didn't matter.

As if her *love* didn't matter.

She drew in another breath. She would get through

this. She had endured much worse in her life than a little heartbreak.

Okay, right now it didn't exactly seem *little*. Still, she would survive.

"Of course," she said stiffly. "I'm sorry. I should have talked to you first. Believe it or not, I had her best interests at heart. Not only do I think she has an amazing voice, but I wanted her to know that even though something terrible has happened to her, her life doesn't have to stop. She doesn't have to cower in a room somewhere, afraid to live, to take any chances. I wanted to show her that she can still use her gift to bring light and music to the world. To bring joy to other people."

The moment she said the words, realization pounded over her like an avalanche rushing down the mountain.

This was what the Sparkle books did for people. It was what *she* did for people. All this time she had felt so uncomfortable with her unexpected success, afraid to relish it, unable to shake the feeling that she didn't deserve it.

She had a gift for storytelling. Her mother and father had nurtured that gift her entire life, but especially when their family had been held captive in Colombia.

Tell us a story, CeCe, her father would say in that endlessly calm voice that seemed to hold back all the chaos. He would start her off and the two of them would spin a new tale of triumph and hope to distract the others from their hunger and fear. She told stories about dragons, about a brave little mouse, about a girl and a boy on an adventure in the mountains.

Tears welled up as she remembered how proud and delighted her parents had been with each story. Maybe that was another reason she'd struggled to accept her Sparkle success, because they weren't here to relish it with her.

Yes, it would have been wonderful. She would have loved to see in the pride in their eyes, but in the end, it didn't matter. Not really. Her sisters were here. They were infinitely thrilled for her, and that was enough.

More important, *she* was here. She had a gift and it was long past time she embraced it instead of feeling embarrassed and unworthy anytime someone stopped her to tell her how much her words meant to them.

"Excuse me," she mumbled to him, needing to get away. Just as she turned to escape, her niece, Louisa, came out of the dressing room holding a book.

"Aunt CeCe, do you know where Olivia went? We were talking about *The Best Christmas Pageant Ever*. She'd never read it, and I told her I got an extra copy at school and she could have it. I want to make sure I don't forget to give it to her."

She turned away from Flynn, hoping none of the glittery tears she could feel threatening showed in her eyes.

"She's probably in the dressing room."

"I don't think so. I just came from there and I didn't see her."

"Are you looking for Olivia?" Barrett asked, joining them from the boy's dressing room. "She left."

She frowned at her nephew even as she felt Flynn tense beside her. "Left? What do you mean, she left?"

He shrugged. "She said she wanted to go see something. I saw her go out the back door. I thought it was kind of weird because she didn't even have a coat on, just her angel costume."

Celeste stared down at the boy, her heart suddenly racing with alarm. The angel costume was thin and not at all suitable for the wintry conditions in the Idaho mountains. Even a few minutes of weather exposure could be dangerous.

"How long ago was this?" Flynn demanded.

"I don't know. Right after we were done singing. Maybe ten minutes."

"She can't have gone far," Celeste said.

"You don't know that," Flynn bit out.

He was right. Even in ten minutes, the girl *might* have wandered into the forest of pine and fir around the ranch and become lost, or she could have fallen in the creek or wandered into the road. In that white costume, she would blend with the snow, and vehicles likely wouldn't be able to see her until it was too late.

Her leg still wasn't completely stable. She could have slipped somewhere and be lying in the snow, cold and hurt and scared...

Icy fingers of fear clutched at her, wrapping around her heart, her lungs, her brain.

"We can't panic," she said, more to herself than to him. "I'll look through the lodge to find her first, and then I'll get Rafe and everyone out there searching the entire ranch. We'll find her, Flynn. I promise."

Chapter Thirteen

He heard her words as if from a long distance away, as if she were trying to catch his attention with a whisper across a crowded room.

This couldn't be real. Any moment Olivia would come around the corner wearing that big smile he was beginning to see more frequently. He held his breath, but she didn't magically appear simply because he wished it.

Cold fear settled in his gut, achingly familiar. He couldn't lose her. Not after working so hard to get her back these past few months.

"We'll find her, Flynn," Celeste said again, the panic in her voice a clear match to his own emotions.

She cared about his daughter, and he had been so very mean to her about it. He knew he had hurt her. He had seen a little light blink out in her eyes at his cruel words.

Her progress or lack of progress is none of your busi-

*ness. She's my daughter. I get to make those choices for
her, not some small-town librarian who barely knows
either of us.*

He would have given anything at that moment to take
them back.

He didn't even know why he had gotten so upset seeing Olivia up onstage—probably because he still wanted
to do anything he could to protect her, to keep her close
and the rest of the world away.

He didn't want her to become like her mother or his,
obsessed with recognition and adulation. At the same
time, he had been so very proud of her courage for standing in front of strangers and singing her little heart out.

None of that mattered right now. She was missing and
he had to find her.

He hurried to find his coat, aware of a bustle of activity behind him as Rafe jumped up, followed by Hope
and Faith.

The instant support comforted him like a tiny flickering candle glowing against the dark night in a window
somewhere. Yeah, they might be temporary visitors in
Pine Gulch, but he and Olivia had become part of a community, like it or not.

Celeste's brother-in-law stopped for an instant to rest
a hand on Flynn's shoulder on his way to grabbing his
own coat off the rack. "Don't worry, man. We'll find her.
She'll be okay."

He wanted desperately to believe Rafe.

He couldn't lose her again.

They would find her.

A frantic five-minute search of the lodge revealed no
sign of one little girl. She wasn't in any of the bathrooms,

the kitchen area, the closed gift shop or sitting beside any of the senior citizens as they enjoyed their meal, oblivious to the drama playing out nearby.

Rafe texted Celeste that he had searched through the barn with no sign of her. Faith and Hope had gone up to the house to see if they could find her there. Rafe told her he wanted to take a look around the reindeer enclosure for a little blond angel next and then head for some of the other outbuildings scattered about the ranch.

As soon as she read the word *angel*, something seemed to click in her brain. Angel. She suddenly remembered Olivia's fascination the other night with the angel above the little chapel in the Christmas village.

Excitement bubbled through her, and she suddenly knew with unshakable certainty that was where she would find the girl.

She grabbed her coat off the rack—not for her, but for Olivia when she found her—and raced outside without bothering to take time throwing it on.

Though Hope and Rafe had elected to close the rest of the ranch activities early that night—the sleigh rides, the sledding hill, the reindeer photography opportunities—because all hands were needed for the dinner and show, they had chosen to keep on the lights at the Christmas village for anyone who might want to stop and walk through it.

She nodded to a few families she knew who were enjoying the village, the children wide-eyed with excitement, but didn't take time to talk. She would have to explain away her rudeness to them later, but right now her priority was finding Olivia.

When she reached the chapel, she nearly collapsed with relief. A little angel in a white robe and silver tinsel halo stood in front of it, hands clasped together as she gazed up at the Madonna, the baby and especially the angel presiding over the scene.

Before she greeted the girl, Celeste took a precious twenty seconds to send a group text to Flynn, her sisters and Rafe to call off the search, explaining briefly that she had found Olivia safe and sound at the Christmas village.

With that done, she stepped forward just in time to hear what the girl was saying.

"Please tell my mom I don't want to be sad or scared all the time anymore. Do you think that's okay? I don't want her to think I don't love her or miss her. I do. I really do. I just want to be happy again. I think my daddy needs me to be."

Oh, Celeste so remembered being in that place after her parents had died—feeling so guilty when she found things to smile about again, wondering if it was some sort of betrayal to enjoy things like birthday cakes and trick-or-treating and the smell of fresh-cut Christmas trees.

She swallowed down her emotions and stepped forward to wrap her coat around Olivia. As she did, she noticed something that made her break out in goose bumps.

"If it means anything," she murmured, "I think your mom heard you."

The girl looked up. Surprise flickered in her eyes at seeing Celeste, but she gave her a tremulous smile and took the hand Celeste held out. "Why do you think so?"

"Look at the star."

Sure enough, the star above the chapel that had been out the other night flickered a few times and then stayed on.

Celeste knew the real explanation probably had to do with old wiring or a loose bulb being jostled in and out of the socket by the wind. Or maybe it was a tiny miracle, a sort of tender mercy for a grieving child who needed comfort in that moment.

"It *is* working," Olivia breathed. "Do you think my mom turned it on?"

"Maybe."

The star's light reflected on her features. "Do you... do you think she'll be mad at me for being happy it's Christmas?"

"Oh, honey, no." Heedless of the snow, Celeste knelt beside the girl so she could embrace her. "Christmas is all about finding the joy. It's about helping others and being kind to those in need and holding on to the people we love, like your dad. I heard what you said to the angel, and you're right. It hurts his heart to see you sad. Dads like to fix things—especially *your* dad—and he doesn't know how to fix this."

"When I cry, he sometimes looks as if he wants to cry, too," she said.

Celeste screwed her eyes shut, her heart aching with love for both of them. She didn't know the right words to say. They were all a jumble inside her, and she couldn't seem to sort through to find the right combination.

When she looked up, the peaceful scene in the little church seemed to calm her and she hugged the girl close to her. "It's natural to miss your mom and to wish she was still with you. But she wouldn't want you to give up things like sleigh rides and Christmas carols and playing with your friends. If that angel could talk, I think that's exactly what she would tell you your mom wanted you to hear."

Olivia seemed to absorb that. After a moment she exhaled heavily as if she had just set down a huge load and could finally breathe freely. She turned to Celeste, still kneeling beside her, and threw her arms around her neck.

That ache in her chest tightened as she returned the embrace, wondering if this would be her last one from this courageous girl she had come to love as much as she loved her father.

"Thanks for letting me be in the show," Olivia said. "It made me really happy. That's why I wanted to come out here, to see if the angel could ask my mom if it was okay with her."

Celeste hadn't known Elise Chandler, but from what little she did know, she had a feeling the woman would love knowing her daughter enjoyed entertaining people.

"I'm glad you had fun," she answered. "Really glad. But you scared everybody by coming out here without telling anyone. In fact, we should probably find your dad, just to make absolutely sure he got the message that you're safe."

"I'm here."

At the deep voice from behind them, she turned around and found Flynn watching them with an intense, unreadable look in his eyes.

Her heartbeat kicked up a notch. How much had he heard? And why was he looking at her like that?

Olivia extricated herself from Celeste, who rose as the girl ran to her father.

Flynn scooped her into his arms and held her tight, his features raw with relief.

"I'm sorry I didn't tell you where I was, Daddy."

"You know that's the rule, kiddo. Next time, you need to make sure you tell me where you're going so I know where to find you."

"I will," she promised.

As he set her back to the ground, her halo slipped a little and he fixed it for her before adjusting Celeste's baggy coat around the girl's shoulders. "I've been worried about you, Livie."

He didn't mean just the past fifteen minutes of not knowing where she was, Celeste realized. He was talking about all the fear and uncertainty of the past three months.

Her love for him seemed to beam in her chest brighter than a hundred stars. How was she going to get through all the days and months and years ahead of her without him?

"I don't want to be sad anymore," Olivia said. "I still might be sometimes, but Celeste said the angel would tell me Mom wouldn't want me to be sad *all* the time."

His gaze met hers and she suddenly couldn't catch her breath at the intense, glittering expression there. "Celeste and the angel are both very wise," he answered. He hugged her again. "You'll always miss your mom. That's normal when you lose someone you love. But it doesn't mean you can't still find things that make you happy."

"Like singing. I love to sing."

He nodded, even though he did it with a pained look. "Like singing, if that's what you enjoy."

The two of them were a unit, and she didn't really have a place in it.

She thought of his words to her. *She's my daughter. I get to make those choices for her, not some small-town librarian who barely knows either of us.*

They stung all over again, but he was right. For a brief time she had been part of their lives, but the time had come to say goodbye.

"Since you're safe and sound now, I really should go,"

she said with bright, completely fake cheer. "Why don't you hurry back to the lodge and change out of your angel costume, then you can grab some dinner?"

"I *am* hungry," Olivia said.

She smiled at the girl, though it took all her concentration not to burst into tears. A vast, hollow ache seemed to have opened up inside her.

"I'm sure Jenna McRaven can find both of you a plate. It all looked delicious."

"Good idea."

"I'll see you both later, then," she answered.

Even though they would be heading in the same direction, she didn't think she could walk sedately beside him and make polite conversation when this ache threatened to knock her to her knees.

Without waiting for them, she hurried back toward the lodge. As she reached it, the lights gleamed through the December night. Through the windows, she saw the dinner still in full swing. Suddenly, she couldn't face all that laughter and happiness and holiday spirit.

She figured she had done her part for the people of Pine Gulch. Let her sisters handle the rest. She needed to go home, change into her most comfortable pajamas, open a pint of Ben & Jerry's and try to figure out how she could possibly face a bleak, endless future that didn't contain a certain darling girl and her wonderful father.

By another Christmas miracle, she somehow managed to hold herself together while she hurried through the cold night to her SUV, started the engine and drove back to the foreman's cottage.

The moment she walked into the warmth of her house, the tears she had been shoving back burst through like a dam break and she rushed into her bedroom, sank onto her bed and indulged herself longer than she should have in a good bout of weeping.

She was vaguely aware that Linus and Lucy had followed her inside and were watching her with concern and curiosity, but even that didn't ease the pain.

While some part of her wanted to wish Flynn had never returned to Pine Gulch so that she might have avoided this raw despair, she couldn't be so very selfish. Olivia had begun her journey toward healing here. She had made great progress in a very short amount of time and had begun regaining all she had lost in an act of senseless violence.

If the price of her healing was Celeste's own heartache, she would willingly pay it, even though it hurt more than she could ever have imagined.

After several long moments, her sobs subsided and she grew aware that Lucy was rubbing against her arm in concern while Linus whined from the floor in sympathy. She picked up both animals and held them close, deeply grateful for these two little creatures who gave her unconditional love.

"I'm okay," she told them. "Just feeling sorry for myself right now."

Linus wriggled up to lick at her salty tears, and she managed a watery smile at him. "Thanks, bud, but I think a tissue would be a better choice."

She set the animals back down while she reached for the box on the table beside her bed.

She would get through this, she thought as she wiped away her tears. The pain would be intense for a while, she didn't doubt, but once Flynn and his daughter returned to California and she didn't have to see either of them all the time, she would figure out a way to go forward without them.

She would focus instead on the many things she had to look forward to—Christmas, the new book release, the movie production, a trip to New York with Hope to meet with their publisher at some point in the spring.

With a deep breath, she forced herself to stop. Life was as beautiful as a silky, fresh, sweet-smelling rose, even when that beauty was sometimes complicated by a few thorns.

She rose and headed to the bathroom, where she scrubbed her face in cold water before changing into her most comfortable sweats and fuzzy socks.

The mantra of her parents seemed to echo in her head, almost as if they were both talking to her like the angels Olivia had imagined. If they were here, they would have told her the only way to survive heartache and pain this intense was to throw herself into doing something nice for someone else.

With that in mind, she decided to tackle one more item on her holiday to-do list—wrapping the final gifts she planned to give her family members. It was a distraction anyway, and one she badly needed. She grabbed the gifts from her office and carried them to the living room, then hunted up the paper, tape and scissors. With everything gathered in one place, she turned on the gas fireplace and the television set and plopped onto the floor.

Lucy instantly nabbed a red bow from the bag and started batting it around the floor while Linus cuddled next to her. She had just started to wrap the first present when the little dog's head lifted just seconds before the doorbell rang.

It was probably one of her sisters checking on her after

her abrupt exit from the dinner. She started to tell them to come in, then remembered she had locked the door behind her out of habit she developed while away at school.

"Coming," she called. "Just a moment."

She unlocked the door, swung it open and then stared in shock at the man standing on the porch. Instantly, she wanted to shove the door shut again—and not only because she must look horrible in her loose, baggy sweats, with her hair a frizzy mess and her makeup sluiced away by the tears and the subsequent cold water bath.

"Flynn! What are you doing here?"

He frowned, concern on his gorgeous features. "You didn't stick around the lodge for dinner. I tried to find you to give your coat back but you had disappeared."

"Oh. Thanks."

She took the wool coat from him, then lowered her head, hoping he couldn't see her red nose, which probably wasn't nearly as cute as Rudolph's.

Though she didn't invite him in, he walked into the living room anyway and closed the door behind him to keep out the icy air. She should have told him not to bother, since he wouldn't be staying, but she couldn't find the words.

"Are you feeling okay?" he asked.

Sure. If a woman who was trying to function with a broken heart could possibly qualify as *okay*. She shrugged, still not meeting his gaze. "It's been a crazy-busy few days. I needed a little time to myself to get ready for Christmas. I've still got presents to wrap and all."

She gestured vaguely toward the coffee table and the wrapping paper and ribbon.

He was silent for a moment and then, to her horror,

she felt his hand tilt her chin up so she had no choice but to look at him.

"Have you been crying?" he asked softly.

This had to be the single most embarrassing moment of her life—worse, even, than crashing her bicycle in front of his grandmother's house simply because she had been love struck and he hadn't been wearing a shirt.

"I was, um, watching a bit of a Hallmark movie a little earlier and, okay, I might have cried a little."

It wasn't a very good lie and he didn't look at all convinced.

"Are you sure that's all?" he asked, searching her expression with an intensity she didn't quite understand.

She swallowed. "I'm a sucker for happy endings. What can I say?"

He dropped his hand. "I hope that's the reason. I hope it's not because you were upset at me for acting like an ass earlier."

She tucked a strand of hair behind her ear. "You didn't at all. You were worried for your daughter. I understand. I was frantic, too."

"Before that," he murmured. "When we were talking about Olivia's solo in the show. I was cruel to you, and I'm so, so sorry."

She didn't know how to respond to that, not when he was gazing at her with that odd, intense look on his features again.

"You were a concerned father with your daughter's best interests at heart," she finally said. "And you didn't say anything that isn't true. I *am* a small-town librarian, and I'm very happy in that role. More important, I don't have the right to make decisions for Olivia without ask-

ing you. I should have told you about her solo. I'm sorry
I didn't."

He made a dismissive gesture. "That doesn't matter.
While she was missing, I prayed that if we found her, I
would drive her myself to acting lessons, singing lessons, tap-dancing lessons. Whatever she wants. As long
as she's finding joy in the world again and I can help her
stay centered, I don't care what she wants to do. She's not
my mother or Elise. She's a smart, courageous girl, and
I know she can handle whatever comes her way. These
past few months proved that."

In that moment she knew Olivia would be fine. Her
father would make sure of it. It was a great comfort amid
the pain of trying to figure out how to go on without
them.

"I realized something else while we were looking for
Olivia," Flynn said. He stepped a little closer.

"What's that?" she whispered, feeling breathless and
shaky suddenly. Why was he looking at her like that, with
that fierce light in his eyes and that soft, tender smile?

Her heart began to pound, especially when he didn't
answer for a long moment, just continued to gaze at her.
Finally, he took one more step and reached for her hand.

"Only that I just happen to be in love with a certain
small-town librarian who is the most caring, wonderful
woman I've ever met."

Nerves danced through her at the words, spiraling in
circles like a gleeful child on a summer afternoon.

"I... You're what?"

His hand was warm on hers, his fingers strong and
firm and wonderful. "I've never said that to anyone else
and meant it. Truly meant it."

She took a shaky breath while those nerves cartwheeled in every direction. "I... Exactly how many other small-town librarians have you known?"

He smiled a little when she deliberately focused on the most unimportant part of what he had said. "Only you. Oh, and old Miss Ludwig, who had the job here in Pine Gulch before you. I think my grandmother took me into the library a few times when I was a kid, and I *definitely* never said anything like that to her. She scared me a little, if you want the truth."

"She scared me, too," she said. *You scare me more*, she wanted to say.

He leaned down close enough that only a few inches separated them. "You know what I meant," he murmured, almost against her mouth. "I've never told a woman I loved her before. Not when the words resounded like this in my heart."

"Oh, Flynn." She gave him a tremulous smile, humbled and awed and deeply in love with him.

He was close enough that she only had to step on tiptoes a little to press her mouth to his, pouring all the emotion etched on her own heart into the kiss.

He froze for just a moment and then he made a low, infinitely sexy sound in his throat and kissed her back with heat and hunger and tenderness, wrapping his arms tightly around her as if he couldn't bear to let her go.

A long while later he lifted his head, his breathing as ragged as hers and his eyes dazed. She was deliriously, wondrously happy. Her despair of a short time earlier seemed like a distant, long-ago memory that had happened to someone else.

"Does that kiss mean what I hope?" he murmured.

She could feel heat soak her cheeks and all the words seemed to tangle in her throat. She felt suddenly shy, awkward, but as soon as she felt the urge to retreat into herself where she was safe, she pushed it back down.

For once, she had to be brave, to take chances and seize the moment instead of standing by as a passive observer, content to read books about other people experiencing the sort of life she wanted.

"It means I love you," she answered. "I love you so very much, Flynn. And Olivia, too. I lied when I told you I was crying over a television show. I was crying because I knew the two of you would be leaving soon, and I…I didn't think my heart could bear it."

"I don't want to go anywhere," he said. "Pine Gulch has been wonderful for Olivia *and* for me. She might have been physically wounded, but I realized while I was here that some part of me has been emotionally damaged for much longer. This place has begun to heal both of us."

He kissed her again with an aching tenderness that made her want to cry all over again, this time because of the joy bubbling through her that seemed too big to stay contained.

She didn't know what the future held for them. He had a company in California, a life, a home. Perhaps he could commute from Pine Gulch to Southern California, or maybe he might want to take Rafe's advice and open a branch of his construction company here.

None of that mattered now, not when his arms and his kiss seemed to fill all the empty corners of her heart.

A long time later, he lifted his head with reluctance in his eyes. "I should probably go find Olivia. I left her with Hope and Rafe at the lodge. I'm sure she's having a great time with the other kids, but I hate to let her out of my sight for long."

"I don't blame you," she assured him.

He stepped away, though he didn't seem to want to release her hands. "I doubt Rafe was buying the excuse when I told him that I needed to return your coat. Something tells me he knows the signs of a man in love."

She could feel her face heat again. What would her family say about this? She didn't really need to ask. They already seemed to adore Olivia, and once they saw how happy she was with Flynn, they would come to love him too.

"Do you want to come with me to pick her up?" he asked.

She wanted to go wherever he asked, but right now she still probably looked a mess. "Yes, if you can give me ten minutes to change."

"You look fine to me," he assured her. "Beautiful, actually."

When he looked at her like that, she felt beautiful, for the first time in her life.

"But if you *have* to change—and if I had a vote—I'm particularly fond of a particular T-shirt you own."

"I'll see what I can do," she answered with a laugh. She kissed him again while the Christmas lights from her little tree gleamed and the wind whispered against the window and joy swirled around them like snowflakes.

Epilogue

"Are you ready for this?"

Celeste took her gaze from the snowflakes outside to glance across the width of the SUV to her husband.

"No," she admitted. "I doubt I will *ever* be ready."

Flynn lifted one hand from the steering wheel to grab hers, offering instant comfort, his calm blowing away the chaotic thoughts fluttering through her like that swirl of snow.

"*I'm* ready," Olivia piped up from the backseat. "I can't *wait*."

"You? You're excited?" Flynn glanced briefly in the rearview mirror at his daughter. "You hide it so very well."

Olivia didn't bother to pay any attention to his desert-dry tone. "This is the coolest thing that's ever happened in my whole life," she said.

Since Olivia wasn't yet a decade old, her pool of experiences was a little shallow, but Flynn and Celeste both declined to point that out.

The girl was practically bouncing in the backseat, the energy vibrating off her in waves. Celeste had to smile. She adored Olivia for the lovely young lady she was growing into.

The trauma of her mother's tragic death had inevitably left scars that would always be part of her, but they had faded over the past two years. Olivia was a kind, funny, creative girl with a huge heart.

She had opened that big heart to welcome Celeste into their little family when she and Flynn married eighteen months earlier, and Celeste had loved every single moment of being her stepmother.

Now Olivia breathed out a happy sigh. "I think I'm more excited about the Pine Gulch premiere of *Sparkle and the Magic Snowball* than the real one in Hollywood tomorrow."

"Really?" Celeste said in surprise. "I thought you'd be thrilled about the whole thing."

Olivia loved everything to do with the film industry, much to Flynn's dismay. Celeste supposed it was in her blood, given her mother's and her grandmother's legacies. Someday those Hollywood lights would probably draw her there, too—something Flynn was doing his best to accept.

"It will be fun to miss school and fly out and stay at our old house. I mean, a movie premiere in Hollywood with celebrities will be glamorous and all. Who *wouldn't* be excited about that?"

In the transitory glow from the streetlights, her features looked pensive. "But I guess I'm more excited about this one because this is our home now," she said after a moment. "This is where our family is and all our friends. Everyone in Pine Gulch is just as excited about the new Sparkle movie as I am, and I can't wait to share it with them."

Oh. What a dear she was. If the girl hadn't been safely buckled in the backseat, Celeste would have hugged her. It warmed her more than her favorite wool coat that her stepdaughter felt so at home in Pine Gulch and that she wanted all her friends and neighbors to have the chance to enjoy the moment, too.

"Good point," Flynn said, smiling warmly at his daughter. "The whole town has been part of the story from the beginning. It's only right that they be the first to see the movie."

"Yep. That's the way I feel," Olivia said.

Her father gave Celeste a sidelong glance before addressing Olivia again. "Good thing your stepmother is so fierce and fought all the way up to the head of the studio to make sure it happened this way. What else could they do but agree? They're all shaking in their boots around her. She can be pretty scary, you know."

Olivia giggled and Celeste gave them both a mock glare, though she knew exactly what he was doing. Her wonderful husband was trying to calm her down the best way he knew how, by teasing away her nerves.

She *had* fought for a few things when it came to her beloved Sparkle character, but wanted to think she had been easygoing. That was what the studio executives had told her anyway. She considered herself extremely fortunate that her vision for the characters and the story matched the studio's almost exactly.

A moment later, Flynn pulled up to the St. Nicholas

Lodge, which had been transformed for the night into a theater.

Somebody—Rafe, maybe—had rented a couple of huge searchlights, and they beamed like beacons through the snowy night. The parking lot was completely full and she recognized many familiar vehicles. Unfortunately, they couldn't fit everyone in town into the lodge so the event had become invitation only very quickly. For weeks, that invitation had become the most sought-after ticket in town.

Though the official premiere the next night in California would be much more of a full-fledged industry event, a red carpet had been stretched out the door of the lodge, extending down the snowy walkway to the edge of the parking lot.

Had that been Faith's doing? Probably. Where on earth had she managed to find a length of red carpet in eastern Idaho? Their older sister was proud of and excited for both Celeste and Hope.

The past two years since they'd signed the contract licensing the Sparkle stories to the animation studio they had chosen to work with seemed surreal. Besides two more bestsellers, they now had a *second* Sparkle animated movie in the works.

Now that she was here, about to walk into the makeshift theater to see people enjoying *her* story come to life on the screen—and it would be enjoyable, she knew, given what she had seen so far of the production—Celeste felt humbled and touched. It didn't seem real that life and fate, her own hard work and her sister's beautiful artwork had thrust her into this position.

"A red carpet," Olivia squealed as she finally noticed— and caught sight of the people lined up in the cold on either side of it, as if this was the real premiere filled with celebrities to gawk over. "How cool is that? That looks like my friend Louise from school. Oh, there's Jose. And Mrs. Jacobs. My whole class is here!"

"I guess you can't escape Hollywood, even here in Pine Gulch," Celeste said quietly to Flynn as he parked in the VIP slot designated for them. "I'm sorry."

He made a rueful face, but she knew him well enough after these deliriously happy months together to know he didn't really mind. He had been her biggest supporter and her second most enthusiastic fan—after Olivia, of course.

"For you, darling, it's worth it," he replied. He tugged her across the seat and pulled her into his arms for a quick kiss. "I'm so proud of you. I hope you know that. I can't wait for the whole world to discover how amazing you are."

Her heart softened, as it always did when he said such tender things to her.

Two years ago, she'd had a pretty good life here in Pine Gulch—writing her stories, working at the library in a job she loved, spending time with her sisters and her niece and nephew and Aunt Mary.

But some small part of her had still been that little girl who had lost both of her parents and was too afraid to truly embrace life and everything it had to offer.

Flynn and Olivia had changed her. At last, she fully understood the meaning of joy. Sparkle might have his magic snowball that could save Christmas, but the true magic—the only one that really mattered—was love.

These past two years had been a glorious adventure—and in seven months, give or take a few weeks, they would all be in for a new turn in their shared journey.

She pressed a hand to her stomach, to the new life

growing there. Flynn caught the gesture and grinned—a secret smile between the two of them. He pressed a hand there as well, then reached for his car door.

"Let's go meet your adoring public," he told her.

She didn't need an adoring public. She had everything she needed, right here, in the family they had created together.

* * * * *

MILLS & BOON®

Cherish™

EXPERIENCE THE ULTIMATE RUSH OF FALLING IN LOVE

215/23

015_MB514

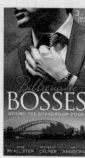
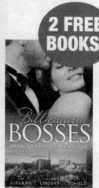

'High drama and lots of laughs'
—*Fabulous* magazine

Fed up with disastrous internet dates and conflicting advice from her friends, Ellie Rigby decides to take matters into her own hands. Instead of looking for a man for herself, she's going to start a dating agency where she can use her extensive experience in finding Mr Wrong to help others find their Mr Right.

Well, that is until a match with one of her clients, charming, infuriating Nick, has her questioning everything she's ever thought about love…

MILLS & BOON